The Picture Game

Best Wishes

Charlie

THE PICTURE GAME

The Picture Game

"Remembering the 1980s can be a bitter sweet experience for many. Thatcher's Briton where the 'Iron Lady' with her famous quote- there is no society and with that the rumbling and pervading attitude of, 'people must look after themselves first'. This is a story about just that, people looking after themselves first. A group of friends trying their best to make ends meet in Coventry City where most of the factory and car industry jobs had vanished.

We follow the lives of a team of mates on The Picture Game, an enterprise comprising of picture sellers going door to door selling factory made pictures, whilst pretending to be art students. The story centres on Cormac and his brother Sean, two brothers who duck and dive their way through a myriad of experiences up and down the country, we get the economic and social reality of the day. Be prepared to encounter the racist and sexist attitudes of the 1980s as Cormac, Sean and their team navigate and ply their trade.

Familial ties, sexuality, exploitation, gender, and issues of race are addressed alongside just the plain ordinariness of life. It's a story told with humour, simplicity, authenticity and is a thought provoking read."

Carol Ann Peters

Copyright © 2020 Charlie McFadden
All rights reserved.
ISBN: 9798644254279

THE PICTURE GAME

**The
Picture
Game**

Charlie McFadden

For Emily.
Nothing without you.

James and Phil, for their encouragement and help.

A big thank you to Linda and Charlie G.

ABOUT THE AUTHOR

Born in Donegal, Ireland, in 1958, Charlie McFadden emigrated to Coventry with his family in the early 1960s. He has worked in a variety of professions, including engineering, the rag trade, property developer, acupuncture practitioner, art gallery owner and picture seller. He now lives in Moreton-in-Marsh, where he is the owner and operator of the Moreton Gallery, a local art gallery.

Foreword

All characters in this book are fictional.

In writing this novel I attempt to provide the reader with an insight into the lives of a gang, who roam the country selling pictures, door to door, by whatever means they can..

I have created characters to reflect the ne'er-do-wells, who like me, made a living on the margins of society.

I apologise for the language which some may find offensive but mean to represent the times, warts and all; raw and unfiltered.

THE PICTURE GAME

1
The Beginnings

Dossers, scallywags, thieves, drug addicts, drug pushers, were all fair game for picture selling. Anyone could try it for a shift or two. If you could sell, you'd made the grade, and were welcomed into the life of a picture seller.

Two-Tone Music was at its peak. The Specials were at number one with Ghost Town. Like many other decaying cities, Coventry and its people were in flux, big industry had gone tits up. The car factories, Jag', Triumph, the Morris, Alvis, Peugeot, once the heart off the city were like weary fighters, the bell had gone for the final round but bloodied and battered, their chances were slim at best. Men and women were scattered to the wind to fend for themselves. Of course, there was always Maggie's starvation rations, a few crumbs thrown their way, by way of the dole but they needed more.

Fancy a half-price TV? Ask a picture seller. A wrap of weed? No problem. Someone giving you problems, and you weren't up to the job yourself? Here's a name of a guy, fifty quid a warning, a hundred and fifty for broken bones. Picture sellers lived in the hinterland between the law and the lawlessness, criminal activity, a kissing cousin. Some invested the profits they made from the pictures into the drugs business, only to either end up in jail or dead. These were the city's Giro 'bates, topping up Maggie's meagre offerings. Through the late 1970s and early '80s, the picture selling business was the primary

THE PICTURE GAME

occupation of Coventry's ne'er- do- wells.

No one was sure who first started it. Some said it was the coming together of Stephen 'Sully' O'Sullivan and Paul 'The One-Eyed Brain' Lucas.

Sully was a larger than life character, originally from Manchester. He was seventeen when he arrived in Coventry, living in doss houses and squats, not staying long in any one place, his volatile nature ensuring a gypsy lifestyle. He made a living through, burglary, shoplifting and pimping. In 1977 he found himself residing at HMP Winson Green, doing a six month stretch for unpaid fines. It was there he met Lucas.

Lucas found himself in The Green after he was stopped with a boot full of spirits paid for on someone else's credit card. He'd run various scams, insurance fraud, chequebooks fraud, credit fraud, anything that would save him doing an honest day's graft. They say he had an IQ of 150, he'd lost his eye after one of his scams went sour, not quite an eye for an eye but it settled the debt.

Sully and Lucas, both came out of the nick at the same time and the probation service set them up on a job selling tea towels and dusters door to door.

It was Sully idea to try a few pictures on their rounds, Lucas was reluctant at first but they took off big. In 1978, they opened a framing and manufacturing factory. It was half the size of a football pitch and produced enough pictures to keep every picture seller in Coventry busy. They had eight teams working for them, travelling up and down the country, moving thousands of pictures a week. Both drove Mercedes sports cars, Sully's red, Lucas' silver, they worked together, socialised together and lived together. Some suggesting their relationship wasn't all business.

It was April 1980 the shit hit the fan, Sully, a thief by nature, was caught with his hand in the till, well actually more like both hands and whatever he couldn't stuff up his jumper, thousand had gone missing. He'd been taking Paul

THE PICTURE GAME

Lucas for a fool and Lucas was no one's fool. Lucas offered him a take it or leave it price for his share of the factory, Sully took it and went on the piss.

Soon teams were setting up all over the city and the game became fiercely competitive with fall outs of one kind or another every week. Six months on, Lucas' factory burnt down. Most thought it was another insurance job, whilst others pointed a finger at Sully. Anyway, Lucas got paid out by the insurance company, upped sticks and bought himself a bar in Spain.

Cormac Finn began his working life as a trainee mechanic but after being made redundant in 1979, he took his place in the dole queue. His friend and neighbour, John Kelly, introduced him to the picture game. John was earning between thirty and sixty quid a night, a lot more money than Cormac was getting on the dole or the factory for that matter.

They worked for Fucked up Freddie, a dark curly-haired garrulous character, full of 'bonhomie.' Although Freddie looked like an extra from a horror movie, his face a mass of scar tissue, left eyebrow missing and jail house tattoos, he was a genuine soft touch, always ready to sub a seller a breakfast, or buy them a drink if they'd had a bum night. Freddie tended to have a high turn-over of sellers, which wasn't helped by his habit of spraying saliva over whoever he spoke to. Besides excessive saliva, Freddie's other flaw was he was hopeless at basic maths. Cormac volunteered to help him out, it didn't take long to figure out where the real money was. By 1982 Cormac had set up his own team, comprising of himself, John, Sean and whoever else was around to fill up the car, the more sellers you take out the more money you bring in. Later he decided he could make far more money making up his own pictures and selling them to other teams.

A year on, Cormac had a very successful business, turning over close to a quarter of a million a year. He had bank accounts in the Irish Republic and Gibraltar. His

THE PICTURE GAME

assembly unit was a former engineering factory that had once produced prop shafts for the now dying car industry. The smell of suds oils the only sign of its former glory. Of red-brick construction it dated back to 1932, and covered eighteen hundred square feet. When they first moved in, it was infested with rats and pigeons. But after four weeks of hard work, it was ready for business.

The front was protected by a huge, black steel-plated door. Once inside and to the left was the storeroom, where the completed pictures were stored, various prints piled high, with a stock list pinned below each shelf. To the right was Cormac's office, which he kept meticulously tidy, locking the office door whenever he was away. A corridor led to the workshop, which was dominated by huge timber worktables in the centre of the room, the assembly line. Below the worktable were stored stock materials, lengths of frame moulding and boxes of prints.

The pictures were prints and sold in three sizes. Smalls, which were five by six inches and went for five or six quid. Mediums, or meds, were twelve by eight inches and sold between eight and a tenner. Meds were the bread and butter of the business. A seller may sell as many as thirty a night, but usually shifted ten to fifteen. The best sellers were birds, owls, falcons and kingfishers. Money wise it was generally a fifty-fifty split between Cormac and the sellers, apart from Big 'Un. Cormac charged fifteen quid for a Big 'Un, usually a map of the world, which measured twenty inches by sixteen. Some had been sold for as much as a hundred quid if the punter was gullible, though on average they usually went for about thirty.

A picture sellers life started generally around midday. Pick-up was anytime between one and three, occasionally from the pub or the dole office but more often from the seller's home. The drive to the shift was biggest part of the job. Knocking doors would begin at about five, and finish around nine. The long drive home could be hard, getting back sometimes after midnight. The conscientious sellers would be dropped off to get their rest whilst for others, the night had just begun.

2
Out on the Shift

Sean flicked the dead bumblebee off the windowsill, watched as it bounced off the side wall, falling onto the lino. He leant down, nudging the corpse with his finger. "Maybe a bit of fresh air will do you good," he picked it up by its glistening wings and flung it out onto the road.

The sky was clear blue apart from a vapour trail left by a plane which had buzzed overhead. Up the road, a red car was parked, blocking the traffic, a white transit van and several other cars were queuing up behind. The van driver and an old man in the red car were arguing.

Sean checked his watch, "They should have been here an hour ago," he thought.

Noticing the door open, Ma wandered over to close it, it was then she spotted Sean standing near the red car.

"What's going on mate?" he called to the driver. You're gonna to have to move."

The old man ignored Sean, his eyes fixed on white van man.

"What's going on?" Ma called over to Sean. "Is there somebody moving in?"

"Nah, I don't think so, I don't know what this guy's doing though, no one can get by." Sean shrugged frustrated, then turned to the old boy, "You're blocking the traffic mate. Come on, move."

Ma shook her head in annoyance.

Sean called to her, "Stan's not normally this late."

THE PICTURE GAME

Ma nodded, she looked proudly towards her son. Where had the years gone, surely it was only yesterday that he was hanging off her apron strings, those brown eyes, that pretty blond head looking up at her. Now look at him, standing up for himself like a man. She smiled to herself. His hair had kept it fairness and he was still as pretty today, as skinny as a stick, but hopefully he'll fill out, she thought. He was eighteen, her baby, but in fact he was a year older than she had been when she married Timmy his father. Jesus, what was she thinking? But who could resist Timmy Finns eyes, dark dreamy pools, darting this way and that, on the lookout for the next pretty girl? He'd had a score of admirers and Ma thought she'd hit the jackpot when he proposed. The girls were all so jealous. She could still remember the sour look on Francis McSorley's face, and the glee on her own as Timmy walked her down the aisle. But the wedding band didn't do anything to change Timmy's ways and it wasn't long after Sean was born that he moved out. It was Sean's older brother Cormac, who was two years older, who'd inherited their father's genes, a tall solid bull of a man, dark, with those same intense eyes.

A large dark cloud was moving in overhead.

"Looks like it's gonna lash down." Sean called over to his mother.

'Rained off,' was a fairly common occurrence on the pictures. Biting cold, howling winds or even snow didn't stop work but rain was a picture seller's nightmare, getting under the glass and ruining the print. Not that the average seller cared too much about the stock. Their only worry was selling pictures, getting pissed and scrounging money for a dinner the following day.

A familiar black Rover mounted the kerb, driving along the pavement, half on and half off. It raced towards them, screeching to an abrupt halt. The driver was Stan, he looked towards Sean, grinning like an imbecile.

"I'll see you later," Sean, pecked his mum on the

7

THE PICTURE GAME

cheek.

The sound of the horn had alerted John Kelly, who lived a few doors down. He hurriedly made his way towards the car.

"Run John, run quick, they'll leave without ya," Ma called, waving a, "Come on, come on!"

John put on a little sprint.

She had a soft spot for John, partly at his simple uncomplicated resolve, which reminded her of Timmy, but also, he carried the name Kelly, her maiden name.

"No chance," he laughed.

Opening the front passenger seat, he winked at Ma. The front seat was reserved for the top seller from the previous night.

Sean was in the back with Sue.

Ma peered in the window at the pretty girl, and smiled and waved as the car pulled off. "Bye now, bye now."

The car reversed back down the street, bumping up onto the kerb and disappeared. Ma was not keen on girls going out on the pictures. Sluts mostly, she thought, she knew the sort alright. "Well, what type of girl would sit in a car surrounded by rowdy lads?"

"Where's Lucy?" John asked.

Stan cackled a phlegmy laugh, rubbing his ginger stubble. With his front teeth missing, his voice was a raspy lisp. His hair was thin and greasy, he was in his mid-thirties but looked a lot older and had been driving pictures teams on and off for years.

"She's not working, I think she's gone back to college," said Stan. "Fuck her, we've got Sue. Ain't that right Sue?"

Sue laughed and slapped Stan playfully on the side of the head. Sue was a lot better-looking than Lucy. Short-cropped blonde hair and voluptuous red lips. She was wearing a figure-hugging blue top and jeans. Sean pressed his nose against her neck.

Stan broke in. "Do you know how long I've been waiting behind those tossers?"

"Twenty-five fucking minutes I was sitting there. The old twat in the car won't move, he's just sitting there. The guy in the van's just nudged into the back of him. Only a tiny knock." He pinched his thumb and forefinger together to emphasis the size of the dent. "Hardly a scratch, but the old bastard won't move until the coppers turn up."

Sue pushed Sean away, glancing across at John, she mouthed, "Bullshit."

They smiled, letting Stan go on.

"This Paki behind me," Stan lisped, "couldn't fucking reverse or speak fucking English either." He glances over his shoulder. "Fucking hopeless! I had to do it for him. I must have looked a right cunt reversing down the road with this raghead standing behind directing me. I should have run the bastard over," he cracked out laughing.

"He thought you were gonna nick his car?" said John, adding, "I wouldn't let you reverse my car," looking to Sue in hope of some appreciation.

Stan cackled again. "A Datsun Cherry, as if I'd run off with a fucking Datsun. A decent car yeah, not a stinking Paki's car, I couldn't wait to get out of it. Honest it stank." He lifted the front of his T-shirt to his nose and sniffed. "Do I smell of Paki?"

"No, you just stink Stan", said Sean. "Fucking B.O mate."

Stan glanced up at his reverse mirror. "They shouldn't give them bastards licence', they shouldn't be on the fucking…" He trailed off, as no-one was taking any notice. "Driving a bunch of tossers."

"What you on about? It's you who ain't got a licence." Sean called from the back of the car.

Stan's eyes flashed. "I have got a licence, I ain't been banned," he said. "It's just I can't use my own."

"Why not?" Sue asked. Her voice was clipped and cultured, a marked contrast to the uncouth banter of the boys. Eight months ago, she'd dropped out of a law degree at Warwick University, bored by the constant essay writing, her parents were furious, hoping she'd return to her studies. But for now, she was enjoying the picture game. She'd had more laughs in the last six months than in her previous five years, and could make decent money too. She elbowed Sean as he ran his hand over her stomach.

"Why not?" blurted Stan, repeating her question, "Yeah, well I could, but…"

"What?" Sue said, leaning forward in her seat.

"It's a long story," replied Stan, mischievously. "I skipped bail five years ago."

"Fuck off, you're full of shit, he ain't even took his test," Sean called out.

"Fuck off yourself," said Stan turning around.

Stan!" John shouted jerking the steering wheel to avoid a parked car. The car spun from one side of the road to the other, tyres screeching in protest. It bounced against the kerbside before skidding to a halt, having turned a full three hundred and sixty. All fell silent before Sue started laughing.

"It's ok I saw it," Stan shouted, "If you didn't pull the fucking steering wheel."

"You didn't fucking see it," John screamed. "You were looking over your shoulder, I fucking saw ya!"

John's neck muscles were taut, a vein showed clearly above his t-shirt collar.

"Watch the road, you fucking idiot," said John.

Stan looked pale. He was breathing heavily, shaking his head defensively as John glared. "I saw it, John, honestly, I did see it," he repeated. "It was you pulling the steering wheel."

John did not speak, but fixed Stan with an icy stare, daring Stan to even glance in his direction. Stan knew better and looked away.

Sue and Sean both giggled.

Stan gripped the steering wheel, his eyes were on the road ahead. He could feel John's glare boring into him, a telegraphed punch waiting to land. "Sorry mate," still unable to face John, "Sorry, mate."

John lowered his gaze, his jaw softened. John was the experienced hand on the job. He was twenty-two years old and when not in borstal or jail had made his legal money from the pictures. His family were one of the largest in the neighbourhood and probably the roughest. Hair slicked back, over a large brick head, a blue dot stained his cheekbone. He had a strong sense of loyalty and if you were his friend, rightly or wrongly, he would provide the muscle. With a natural swagger, he could hold his own.

The window wipers drummed out a rhythmic beat on the dashboard, rain the scattered melody. Taking the ring-road, they headed north on the Birmingham road, stopping at a set of traffic lights. Sean watched as people huddled together beneath a bus shelter. About twenty yards on a young woman scrambled to cover her baby as the rain lashed down. She was about twenty, slim with auburn hair. Her thin cotton dress was sheer and flimsy, clinging to her like a mischievous pervert.

"Look, look!" Sean said.

"Whoa! She's fucking naked," replied John. "Fucking hell, look at her tits, look at them."

Sue leant forward.

Windows down they ogled as the rain continued its onslaught. The lights changed, a car behind blared its horn. Stan selecting first gear and at a snail's pace moved off.

"Get your tits out!" shouted John.

The girl momentarily looked up.

"Get 'em out let's have a look at them," shouted Sean. He turned to Sue, pulling at her jumper. "Come on, get 'em out!"

Sue turned towards the window, her arms covering her chest, slapped him. "Get off me, you get your dick out," with a look of, I dare you.

John leant across from the front seat, eyeing Sue, "What's going on, you getting stirred up?"

"Fuck off the lot of you, that's enough now," said Sue.

THE PICTURE GAME

"That's enough," Her voice was sharp and hard.

Sean tried once more but got a firm slap in his face for his efforts. "You bitch, fucking hell I was only having a bit of fun!" Sean said retreating, "Stuck up cow."

"You fuck off yourself," Sue raised her eyes disapprovingly, then turned looking out the window.

Twenty minutes later they were on the M6, heading north. Sean had fallen asleep on to Sue's shoulder. She pulled a face as she nudged his head off her. Sue was nineteen, and despite her protestations had a massive crush on Sean. She was a good-looking girl and liked the fun and mischief of working the pictures. Once she'd had a drink, Sean could get her to do anything, a blowjob, or even a shag on the way home, sometimes covered over with a coat, sometimes not.

"Where did you say we're going?" asked John.

"Towards Manchester, Sandbach," said Stan, "The weather forecast says it's okay up there. I done it maybe two years ago with the Heatons, we had a real good hit. I reckon it's due…" his voice trailed off.

"I've done Sandbach," Sean said, waking up and yawning. "About six months ago. Good! We only did it for one night though." He stretched and turned smiling at Sue, she put an arm around him, with a playful kiss.

"Whereabouts did you go?" Stan asked tapping out a tune on the steering wheel.

"We just hit the first estate off the M6," John answered. "I remember doing a pub, they loved them. There was a curry house right next to it."

Stan replied, "Yeah, I know it, straight in off the motorway, the pub's right in the middle of the estate, a massive car park out front." Adding. "We sold out there a couple of years ago, Mickey Wilson sold a ton of pictures."

"He's a good seller, Mickey," replied John.

"He's over in Holland now," said Stan. "Amsterdam, too much into his dope." Stan went on, "That curry house,

12

THE PICTURE GAME

the one you're on about, the waiters dress up like Maharajahs."

He glanced towards the back, "It's like you're in fucking India."

Sue disentangled herself from Sean, leaning forward she put her elbows on the back of the driver's seat. "Stan, what did you jump bail for?"

With the mention of jumping bail, Stan's stock had risen, perhaps he wasn't just the goony bloke with a lisp who drove.

Stan was about to turn to speak, but noticing John. "Oh, nothing much, a bit of this and that," his eyes fixed on the road ahead.

"What do you mean, this and that?" she asked, poking her finger into his shoulder.

Despite Stan's unwholesome looks, she was adopting a playful flirting manner. Stan looked up at the mirror grinning.

"Come on, tell me, what's this and that." She persisted. "Are you a secret gangster Stan?"

"He flashed at a twelve-year-old girl in the park," Sean said laughing. "He's a dirty old man; always in the park with his dick out. Loves watching the little girlies flashing their knickers on the swings."

"Fuck off, I'm not a nonce, you're a fucking nonce," Stan shouted.

"You do look like a nonce though Stan." Sean laughed as he sat back in his seat. He knew that despite Stan's bluster, he wouldn't do anything.

Sue looked across at Sean as she evaluated Stan's response.

"You better shut your mouth, or you might fucking regret it." Stan continued.

His manner was challenging, goading Sean.

"Ooh, I'm scared the nonce might get me, mummy," said Sean. He waved his hands in mock fear, closed his eyes, his tongue stuck out the side of his mouth as he pretended to masturbate. "Just a little higher girlie, go on, just a little higher."

Sue laughed.

Stan glared back at Sean, "Oh, fucking brave." Then, changing tack. "Looks as if you've done that before," laughing. "Don't let your kids near that fucker!" he glanced around in hope of support, knowing he was wasting his time getting angry. Sean was the darling of the team and could do whatever he wanted. Money was not a motivating factor for Sean, Cormac paid him two hundred quid a week whether he sold a picture or not. If it weren't for his brother and John, he would have been off the team after the first week.

John looked across, "Just drive the fucking car Stan," then to Sean, "Someone's gonna fill that mouth of yours one day." He winked at Stan, who smiled at the tit-bit thrown his way.

Stan put his foot down and was hitting close to ninety, right up the backside of the car in front. Speed and dangerous driving were prerequisites in being a picture seller driver. A lot were ex-car thieves and joyriders, who loved the thrill of speed. They generally drove as fast as the car and traffic would go. All the cars were rentals, lasting a couple of years before either blowing up, or being written off. The lads in the car hire place knew the score but didn't mind if you signed up for another.

Sean checked his watch as a red Volvo moved alongside. It was being driven by a midget. He was about to make a joke, when the midget smiled. Sean smiled back embarrassed, and turned away. Sue had placed her elbows on the driver seat, she whispered something in Stan's ear. Stan nodded and mutter something back, she giggled, and gently flicked his hair.

THE PICTURE GAME

3
Dropping off at Sully's

Saturday August 15th, it was Sully's birthday and Cormac had agreed to drop him out a delivery. In the van were Sean, John and himself and as they pulled up outside the workshop, Cormac was wary. Sully could be unpredictable, particularly when hc had a drink in him. Cormac reminded himself to expect the unexpected. Sean had wheeled in the pallet truck, he had a simple rule on stock, only he or Sean could book it in, or out. Cormac glanced across at a stack of pictures neatly piled up on a wooden pallet, "That's his order.

Opening the back of the van, Sean climbed in, checking off the order as they loaded.

Cormac made his way to the office to do the paperwork. Sean finished loading and followed his brother.

"That's one hundred and twelve meds, fifty-eight smalls, and thirty big-uns," said Sean looking up, as he took out the first aid kit from the desk. He stuck a plaster over his thumb. "I've cut myself on one of those staples, I'm always doing that." He peeled back the plaster to reveal a deep oozing cut.

"Get out," said Cormac, shoving his brother, "you're making a mess."

A large drop of blood splashed down onto the oak desk.

"Get a cloth; you're bleeding all over the place," Cormac said as he moved the paperwork to one side of the

15

desk.

"Ahh!" Sean lunged forward waving his thumb at Cormac's face, chasing his brother around the desk.

"Fuck off, you dirty bastard, you're disgusting," said Cormac, slamming the door as he ran from the office.

Sean laughed chasing after him with his blood-stained thumb.

Ten minutes later, they were in the Ford transit belting down the A46 towards Stratford. Cormac checked his watch, it was twelve forty-five, they still had plenty of time, so he dropped his speed down to sixty.

Sean was asleep next to John by the passenger window. John was fiddling with the radio.

"Bloody hell it's hot," said Cormac. He lifted the front of his T-shirt to catch the breeze from the open window. "A bit of air mate, I reckon it's got to be one of the hottest days, the sweats pissing out of me." He put his hand through the open window directing the cooling breeze towards his face.

John leant across Sean, lowering the window on the passenger's side. "That fucker asleep already."

Sean's body weaved gently back and forth with the motion of the road. He opened his eyes briefly, as the wind hit his face, readjusted his position and dropped back into his slumber.

Shaking his head Cormac smiled over at his brother, he picked up a pack of cigarettes off the dashboard. "Some man he is, he could sleep on top of a pole." Handing the pack to John, "Light us one up, will you mate?"

He was more at ease with John coming along, who'd won far more arguments with his fists than his intellect, so there were no worries if Sully played up. They pulled up into the car park of a large Victorian pub just off the main Stratford road. The front was covered with hanging baskets, dripping wet after just being watered.

"I'm sure this is it," said Cormac pulling on the handbrake. "The first pub after the island is what he said."

THE PICTURE GAME

Once out of the van, Cormac stood for a moment scrutinising Sully's delivery note before handing it to Sean. "Have a quick look at that, I don't want him pulling me up," Cormac stood over his shoulder as Sean rechecked the figures.

Sean gave him a look, saying, "What the fuck, stop breathing down my neck."

Cormac backed off.

"Yeah it's fine," he said confidently, handing the list back.

Cormac, rechecked to satisfy himself once more. He locked the van, clapping his hands as they walked towards the pub. "I'll get them in."

Sitting below a window were an elderly couple in their overcoats despite the heat, they were surrounded by bags of shopping. At one end of the bar, perched on a stool, was a pockmarked faced man of about fifty, he as the boys entered glanced up from his crossword puzzle and took a sip from his pint. Leaning with their backs against the bar, were a couple of black guys. One, well over six feet tall, powerfully built, a head the size of a lion with dreadlocks halfway down his back. The other was much smaller, darker skinned, with sharp eyes.

During the 1960s the majority of immigrants arriving in Britain were Irish, Jamaicans and Indians. Maybe it was their love of music, or their shared outlaw lifestyle. Or maybe it was the 'No Blacks, No dogs, No Irish,' signs commonly seen in pubs and guest houses that cemented a sometimes uneasy alliance between the black and Irish communities.

John and Leroy Philips were friends. They had shared prison and borstal cells, partners in crime, you could say. It was lion headed Leroy who looked over.

"Bloody hell, what the fuck! I thought you were still locked up mate," John laughed as they approached the pair.

Leroy grinned and nudged his friend Murphy, calling

17

out, "We don't have any rowdy Irish in our pub," pointing towards the entrance. "Get yourselves back to Paddy land, we don't need no thick mick bums in here, it's a respectable establishment." His smile was broad.

John smiled, "How are you?" he slapped his hand into his friend's fist. "It ain't fussy if it's got two niggers propping up the bar."

John and Leroy embraced.

Cormac interrupted the love in with, "You guys want a drink?"

Leroy's face lit up, "Cheers mate, lager for me," then slapping Murphy's shoulder. "Rum and coke Murph', yeah?"

Murphy knocked back his drink, slamming the empty glass on the bar.

No one remembered how a Melvin Sparks, got the name Murphy, but it stuck. He was known as a part-time D.J come drug pusher.

"What you doing over here?" John asked Leroy.

"Sully's got his party tonight and me and my man are taking care of it," Leroy replied.

"Fucking off, you two! Piss ups in breweries springs to mind," joked John.

Cormac passed out the drinks.

"Cheers," said Leroy raising his glass, head and shoulders above the rest of the group. He put a hand on Johns shoulder and stood back, "You looking a bit heavy man. You could do with getting back in nick, lose a few pounds." He grabbed a roll of flesh on John's waistline. "Too much curry and chips."

John had always been fit, training in the boxing gym four nights a week. A year ago, in settling an argument, he cracked a knuckle and a bone in his right hand, it was in plaster for three months. On his return to the gym, it went again whilst hitting the heavy punch bags, since then he'd stopped training. With no exercise his stomach was expanding by the week.

THE PICTURE GAME

"I can't seem to do fuck all about it," John lifted his shirt, exposing his pale, flabby white stomach, grabbing a fistful. "You niggers don't put it on."

"We don't eat all that shit you fuckers eat, too much chips with your Irish stew. Chicken rice and peas, you won't get a gut like that," laughed Leroy, poking John's stomach with his finger. He lifted the front of his shirt to reveal a well-honed six-pack, pulling up Murphy's shirt to show the same. "Chicken rice and peas man, none of this stew and ten dumplings."

"Don't you be knocking Mrs Kelly's cooking, or she'll be down here to sort you out." John laughed. "You're just lucky, the man upstairs gave us looks and brains and you fuckers, dicks and muscles. You lot just don't get bellies."

Egged on by Cormac and Murphy, Leroy and John continued their piss taking. Sean had wandered off to try his hand on the one arm bandit. All of a sudden, Leroy's nose twitched, he looked over to Murphy who was laughing quietly to himself.

"Can you smell cabbage?" Leroy said, covering his face. "Fucking hell, what's that stink?"

Murphy was shaking his head, his shoulders were shaking as he tried to suppress a laugh.

Leroy looked in severe pain, "Come on, one of you lot have either been spraying on cabbage water or bathing in it? Wah, that fucking stinks!"

A putrid smell of rotten vegetation had engulfed the whole area. Wafting his newspaper under his nose, the man with his crossword moved away.

John pointed at Murphy. "It's that dirty bastard, look at him, he's snuck one out, he's shit his pants, he has!"

Murphy was finding it difficult to control himself, with tears of laughter running down his face.

Cormac had moved alongside Sean to a safe distance. Leroy was overcome, standing stone still, not daring to remove his hand from his nose.

John pushed the laughing Murphy towards the door.

THE PICTURE GAME

"You dirty bastard, fucking get out of here. He has, he's shat himself," he manhandled Murphy out the front door. "You're rotten man, you're fucking rotten."

Murphy tried to come back in but was thrown out three more times by John. After five minutes of complaining and banging on the windows the air had cleared sufficiently to allow him to re-join them.

Twenty minutes later, in walked Sully. Cormac scanned his face, he looked stone-cold sober. By his side strode a beautiful half-caste girl, her features were fine with flawless skin, she was tall, probably five foot ten or eleven, with long slender legs and wore her hair in an afro. Sully introduced her as Veronica. She wore sequined hot pants and a purple and red tie-dye shirt, loosely tied in front.

Sully would be best described as 'black Irish, pale skin, with jet black hair. He said he could trace his family back to Don Juan Miguel Fernandez, his ancestor who landed up in Ireland after the defeat of the Spanish Armada. He was an inch or so shorter than Veronica, and wore his hair tied back in a pony tail. He was wearing Levi's and a ban the bomb T-shirt. The pair could well have been models arriving for a fashion shoot. They smiled making their way over. After getting a drink she suggested they all sit down in the corner by the door.

Sully whispered something to Cormac and they left to transfer the pictures from the Transit to Sully's Volvo estate. Whilst unloading Sully asked Cormac if he had any plans for the evening, saying that he should come over later for his party. Cormac thought for a moment and said yeah, he'd bring Sean and John along too. Sully handed over eight hundred and thirty-five pounds. A smiling Cormac gave him back fifty quid for a birthday drink. Sully looked surprised by Cormac's generosity.

"You're a decent man, there's not many who'd do that," said Sully. He grabbed Cormac around the neck and embraced him. "Tonight, we'll have a great time." He held

THE PICTURE GAME

on to Cormac shoulders and looked him in the face, "You're some man, I had you down as a right tight arse. Fifty quid!"

"I know, I'm regretting it already," laughed Cormac.

"Listen mate if there is anything I can do for you, just let me know," Sully had charm by the truckload.

They locked up their vehicles and returned to the pub. Sully bought the next round, Cormac carried them over and sat alongside his brother.

Sully looked across, "Definitely get over it's gonna be a great night. Murphy's doing the music, aren't you matey?"

"Yeah," said Murphy, "Guaranteed!" He swung his hand making a clicking sound with his fingers.

"How do you do that?" Sean asked.

Murphy showed him, but Sean couldn't get to do it. Veronica laughed, saying it was a black thing, not for whiteys, Sean tried one more time.

Murphy was now clicking his fingers like a football rattle.

Veronica laughed a weird hic-upy laugh.

The glasses were piling, Cormac was on his fifth when he glanced at the clock, it was twenty past four. "We'd better be off." nodding at Sean and John.

They swilled back their beers.

"Okay, let's hit the road," said John.

Leroy had gotten to his feet to embrace his old friend. "Are you coming over tonight?" he asked, knowing John was usually reluctant to stray far from home.

Sully's head shifted to one side waiting for John's response.

"Yeah, definitely," said John.

"Definitely," Leroy repeated, holding on to John's hand.

Definitely, definitely, John replied.

4
On the Doors

It was five o'clock when they pulled into a quiet Cul-de-Sac to set up. Sean laid out the sets, creating three piles, one for each seller. At the bottom were a selection of nine medium pictures, stacked on top of those were ten smalls, and each seller had one large picture.

It was the driver who was responsible for the stock, so he usually kept a close eye on the setting up. A dishonest seller might slip a couple of pictures under the car, helping himself once the driver was out of sight, but Sean was trustworthy. Once set up was complete, sellers got back in the car with a stack of pictures on their knee, ready to be dropped off.

Where they hit or knocked was called 'Prop,' and usually divided into three categories, council, new estate or established (Victorian terraced houses). Big expensive houses were very rarely bothered with. The bread and butter were working class people who were earning. Once out of the car the seller would work their way around the prop, always following the pavement, that way the driver could always find them. A scutterer was a seller who would skip back and forth, selecting only the best houses from both sides of the road. These sellers would steal other seller's sales, often the cause of fights.

Stan drove to a council estate, most of which had been bought by the tenants. This meant weekly cash, without too many commitments, perfect for a picture seller. He

THE PICTURE GAME

pulled up at the side of the road, the two boys got out. Sue wound down the window shouting good luck. In a flash, John was on the other side of thc road, whilst Sean was still getting himself organised.

John had knocked his first door and was on to his second.

"Get a move on," he called over.

Sean slung his Big Un' over his back like a haversack and started up the path to his first house. The door had a recent coat of varnish with a pretty stain glass insert, a good sign. His approach was casual and relaxed, not the toe jam style of your average door to door salesman. He composed himself and rang the bell, stepping away he turned his back, ensuring the home owner first view was of the Big Un'. At the sound of the door opening, he waited then turned, presenting the sincerest smile, he could muster.

"Sorry to disturb you, I'm an art student; we're in the area promoting some of our artwork. I wonder if you have got the time to have a quick look," As he talked, he passed over a pictures to the homeowner, a peregrine falcon.

The blond middle aged lady looked momentarily confused but took the picture. She studied it for a second or two, Sean handed over another. She took that too, holding it away from her body to admire. Placing one foot in the door to prevent it from closing, she ducked inside calling to her husband.

"Colin…. Colin, come here," she shouted.

Adept at handling a set of pictures, Sean could practically juggle them; he made them appear awkward and heavy.

"Do you mind if I put them down for a second," he said.

"Yes, please do," she replied.

As the pictures began slipping this way and that. Sean dropped to one knee, grimacing in his attempts to hold on to the 'awkward' pile.

THE PICTURE GAME

"No, bring them in luv," she said, stepping forward to help. "Don't stand there on the doorstep." She shouted again, louder than previously. "Colin, it's an art student, he's got some paintings to look at."

"Thanks," said Sean as he purposefully wiped his feet on the doormat mat.

"Excuse the light, the bulb's just gone this evening," said the lady in a broad northern accent.

The hallway was dim, the only bit of light was from a mirror on the wall beneath which stood a cabinet with porcelain figurines of ballerinas choreographed into a dance troupe. A plaster statue of a Saint Bernard dog stood by the side, as though guarding over his troupe.

"And the smell, we've just had our dinner," she said, closing the kitchen door. "If you'd been five minutes earlier, I could have set a plate out for you," she laughed.

Passing the mirror, she checked the sides of her mouth for signs of leftovers.

"Now, I'm Gail and him indoors, Colin," she said.

"I'm Sean," said Sean.

She led him through to the lounge. The smell of curry had filled the house, Sean's favourite. The odour tickled and teased his tummy, which rumbled but to no avail.

Colin skipped his feet off a pouffe and turned to face his visitor, annoyed at being disturbed as he tidied the paper which had fallen from his chest. "What's he got?" he asked bluntly.

Gail looked at Colin, her face scolding, then smiling back at Sean, shaking her head apologetically before handing Colin the picture of the falcon. "He's got some beautiful pictures for us to look at. He's from the college, he's a student." She smiled at Sean.

Colin, who was dressed in a short-sleeve shirt and a pair of grey baggy arsed joggers, took the picture. He studied it and then looked up at his wife, who grinned broadly back.

"He's a bird watcher. He'll love them," she said.

THE PICTURE GAME

"You've come to the right house. Anything with birds in it."

Sean made his way to the front of the room. "Is it ok if I put them down here?"

"You can put them down anywhere you like mate," said Colin, obviously not cowed by his wife's reprimand.

Sean placed the set onto the carpet in front of Colin, who moved his feet to one side. Unlike his wife's cheery disposition. Colin was deadpan and monotone, his face pale and expressionless.

"Can I get you a drink luv, a cup of tea Sean?" said Gail.

"No, I'm fine, but thanks anyway," replied Sean.

"A squash, I've got some orangeade in the fridge?"

Sean had made a conscious decision never to accept snacks or drinks. The reason being, it was usually the lady of the house that offered, and it was usually the lady of the house who made the decisions, less distractions the better was his policy.

"No, I'm fine," he insisted.

Sean began his spiel, explaining that they were from the Lanchester College in Coventry and that every now and again they sold off their art coursework to bring in much-needed funds back to the college. He said this, despite the fact they were prints produced by the thousand in a factory in Bedford. He went on to say they were acid etchings and produced in stages, each stage taking a day or two, the whole thing taking as long as a week to make.

The blag had made an impression on Gail, who nudged her husband.

If Sean was ever asked if they were originals, he'd say they were limited to ten. That way, it wasn't a big deal if you sold their neighbour the same picture. The philosophy was to keep things vague, less likelihood of any comeback. Some sellers blag was way over the top, one or two saying the pictures were produced by disabled children living in a hospice, whilst others would scribble off a dedication with a copied signature on the back. Bullshit flew thick and fast in the picture game.

"What other birds have you got?" Colin asked, as he pawed through the stack.

Sean reached over, pulling a pair from the pile. "We've got these two, The Tawny and The Barn Owl. "If you get them in the right light, they look fantastic."

Sean took them to the sunlit chimney breast, holding up the silvery prints, one lower than the other, he gently moved them, they shimmered and sparkled in the sunlight.

"Oh, they do look good," drawled Gail. "Do you mind holding those up as well." She handing him the falcons.

Sean held all four, two in each hand, now and again giving them a delicate flick.

Gail raised her voice, "Colin, help him. Ooh, they really catch the light there?"

Colin went over, pausing as he examined one.

Sean watched nervously as he took it to the window. He was worried that Colin may know that the pictures were cheap prints, knocked out by the thousand. If rumbled, they would have to move out of the area to play it safe. Occasionally the police were called and a few sellers had even been done for fraud.

Sean had a lot of nervous energy and when stressed he would bite his finger nails, he did this now.

"They look alright, good detail on the wings." Colin held it up on the opposite side of the chimney.

"They match your wallpaper," said Sean relieved, as the lump in his chest dissipated.

"They do, I like them." She turned to her husband, "Do you, like them?" before Colin had time to answer, added, "Your mum would love these; she's got something like them in her hallway already. What do you think?"

"How much are they?" Colin replied, playing his cards close to his chest.

"This size," Sean said, holding up a med', "We sell at the college for twenty pounds, but when we're clearing

THE PICTURE GAME

them out, we sell them for ten pounds." Hoping he hadn't pitched too high, he waited for a response.

Gail picked up one or two more, showing them to her husband.

At this stage, Sean could not tell if he was going to be successful or not. He decided it best to give them the silent treatment. It was John who told him about the silent treatment.

"If you're not sure, let 'em stew. But once you're in, pack up quick, don't give them a chance to talk themselves out of it."

He spread the whole set out almost covering their floor and began handing them silently to Gail, one by one.

"I ain't seen nowt like em. How do you make 'em?" Colin asked, his Lancashire accent now evident. "Look at this," He flicked the silvery print as it shimmered in the sunlight.

Sean's confidence was building, he drummed out once more his standard bogus artistic procedure. They learnt about etching, neutralizing, multiple ink processes, polishing, and even how it was framed, as much detail as possible to add as much value. Their faces by the end of his spiel displayed their hand. He had them hooked.

"I can see they've taken some time, just looking at the detail on feathers." Colin, his manner had softened. He turned to his wife, "Have a look at this wing Gail, look at the feathers, they must take bloody ages."

Sean watched as they went through the set, each time coming back to the birds. Sean went quietly to the back of the room where he had propped up his Big Un', the map of the world. "This one would take you the best part of ten days to do."

Colin looked up at the Big 'Un, which knocked him back a couple of feet, with his mouth agape. Sean handed it to him.

Colin's eyes squinted as he scanned it. "How much?" he asked, hook jammed firmly in his jaw.

27

THE PICTURE GAME

"What would you think?" Sean asked.

Colin looked annoyed at the question. He tapped the gold gilt frame with his knuckle, returning to the window to examine it in the light. Gail put down a couple of pictures she was looking at and joined her husband, her bottom lip protruded as she too assessed its value.

"What do you think Luv?" Colin quietly asked his wife, his tone business-like.

"I don't know there's a lot of work in it. I'm hopeless at these things," she replied.

"No, but do you like it? Colin locked eyes with his wife.

"Oh, I love it," she responded.

Colin glanced across at Sean, annoyed at his wife's obvious enthusiasm.

"Hold it over the fireplace," Gail said. She walked to the back of the room, hands on her hips, head to one side, and then the other.

Sean volunteered to help, knowing if the price was right, he'd sold it, but could see that guessing the price was confusing the issue. "You stand back."

Colin joined his wife.

"At college, if we are commissioned, we'll do them from two hundred quid upwards, but it won't be exactly like this. These we do as regular coursework, so we're a bit faster." He looked across, wondering where to pitch his price, they hadn't yet agreed to buy a single picture yet, he thought. He usually charged thirty quid, but as it was the beginning of the night and there was a chance he'd sell it elsewhere, he'd decided to risk it. "We only charge forty-five pounds, but that's only because we need to clear them out," he waited.

"Forty-five quid, that's good value," Gail said, surprise lighting up her face. "I thought you were gonna say a hundred. Honestly! I thought he was gonna say a hundred quid." She nodded across at her husband.

"Well as I said, if you wanted to commission one it

would cost you at least a couple of hundred," Sean said, cursing quietly to himself.

Ten minutes later, with numerous different combinations held on different walls. Gail and Colin decided to buy both sets of birds and the large world map.

"That works out to eighty-five pounds for all five," Sean said.

Gail wrote out the cheque. As he left, Sean thanked them again, Gail wished him well with his studies and made him promise, if he was ever in the area with any new paintings, especially of birds, to call in. At the bottom of the path, he turned to see her cheery face wave him goodbye.

He looked down the road to see if he could spot John, but he was nowhere to be seen. Excited that he had already made himself over fifty quid, he started up the next path. There was no one home, nor in the one after. He picked up pace as he moved on, this time a grumpy old man asked him why he was calling at this time of the night and slammed the door in his face. Sean was used to this, but it still upset him enough to trample over some of the old geezer's plants at the bottom of the garden. Twenty minutes later and no more sales, he heard the familiar parp of the car horn, as Stan pulled up to the kerbside.

"Got rid of your Big 'Un?" Stan called out.

"Yeah, and four meds. Falcons and owls," Sean beamed as he waited at the back of the car.

Stan got out and adjusted the waistband of his trousers. "Falcons and owls," Stan repeated as he opened the boot.

"And a Big 'Un," said Sean.

Sean looked in. There were no Big Uns left, usually they'd be a spare for each seller. Sean checked the back seats, to see if they'd been stacked there. "Where have they all gone?" he asked.

"Sue's sold the fucking lot," said Stan, laughing. He flicked through the prints, pulling out the owls and falcons.

Sean walked to the front passenger door to look inside,

just in case Stan was winding him up. "Honest?"

"She's sold them," said Stan.

Sean turned away shaking his head.

Stan couldn't hide his glee, "Yeah, she sold the fucking lot. Four in one call, and then five minutes later another two, she's had John's too," he spluttered.

"Fucking hell!" Sean said, trying to quickly calculate what she had made up to now. "Fuck's sake," he cursed to himself, "That's buggered it, fucking hell."

She's top seller, sitting next to me tonight," said Stan. He flicked out a yellow tongue, licking the air as he slammed the boot closed. "You lads are gonna have to get a move on."

"How's John doing?" Sean, wondering if he was bottom seller.

"I don't know what he's on, fuck all when I got the Big 'Un off him." Wincing, Stan hitched up his trousers. "My back's killing me; it's all this frigging driving." He let out a sigh. "I gotta get to the doctor." He gingerly eased himself into the car. "Fuck's sake!"

"See you later," said Sean.

Stan drove off without reply.

After seeing how much Stan was struggling, Sean decided to do a few stretching exercises, touching his toes, and twisting his upper body back and forth before setting off. An hour or so later, Sean had only sold another three measly pictures: two small badgers, and a barn owl. After a good start, it had gone downhill rapidly. He checked his watch; it had gone eight already. The next door he knocked, was opened by a pleasant lady who invited him in. Once inside she introduced her daughter, both were redheads. Sean felt sure the daughter was giving him the eye, and it was her who bought a set of gold country scenes. About four doors later, he was invited in and greeted like an old friend. The house was owned by an eccentric looking grey-haired man, earrings and a ponytail. His house was full of birds, all budgerigars, who twittered nonstop as Sean was giving his blag. The old guy told Sean that he always buys pictures off the college students, proudly taking Sean on a tour of his house. Every wall was covered in foil prints with hardly a gap to see the wallpaper. The only ones he didn't have were the two fairy-tale fantasy scenes, Mr Mole, and Alice in Wonderland. He bought both for eight quid apiece. Sean smiled to himself as he waved goodbye.

On he went, the odd picture here and there. The dregs of sunshine had given up on the day and fallen to the ground. Sean had had enough too. His checked his watch, it was a quarter to nine, "Only fifteen minutes left," he thought.

As soon as he knocked on the next door, he knew he shouldn't have. The door frame had been painted so roughly that at least an inch of black paint covered the bubble glass insert. The whole house looked unkempt with a mass of dead flies and wasps scattered on the windowsill. The front garden was a mass of overgrown weeds, a stranded old motorbike a prisoner of the brambles. He prayed that no one would answer, but just as he turned to leave, he heard a rumbling sound of something moving. A blurred white shape flashed into vision behind the door, followed by a loud snuffle. Sean squinted and took a step back.

A man's voice called out, "Back, Dolly, back!"

Sean witnessed what seemed to be a wrestling match between the two. He could hear grunts from both parties with the white blob appearing to be getting the better. He took a couple more steps back, wondering if he should just leave.

"I'll be there in a second." The man called out gruffly.

"Get back," and a sharper, "Get in there, you bastard!"

The blurred denim covered backside of the man was large against the glass, as were his tattooed covered arms. The man grappled for control of the beast and just when it seemed he had control, the beast broke loose, the battle

THE PICTURE GAME

was in full swing again.

Sean squinted but could not decide if it was a dog or a pig.

"Bloody Hell! Get in there, Dolly, you nuisance.

Suddenly there was a sharp sound, a crack flashed across the glass.

"You've broke the fucking glass!" screamed the man.

There was a dull thud, followed by a sharp squeal, or perhaps it was a yelp. Sean did not wait, turning on his heels he ran as fast as he could, only stopping as he turned the corner. He waited a second or two before peeking back around. The huge beast was peeing against a lamp post, a massive Hells Angel was looking up and down the road as he was trying to drag it back indoor.

Sean knocked one or two more but with no luck. It was now dark, he sat down on the side of the road waiting for Stan. Picking up a stick, he scraped it over his shoes taking off the shine. A door opened opposite, it was Indian man putting out his milk bottles. The man looked over and nodded, Sean nodded back. The man walked to the bottom of his garden, closed his gate and stood eyeballing Sean, before returning to his house. A moment later he appeared again at the window before disappearing.

After five minutes of waiting, Sean walked back towards the corner just in case the Indian guy would get paranoid enough to phone the police. As he waited, he made a quick count of his remaining stock, trying to figure out his total. A familiar set of headlights appeared at the end of the road, the left side brighter than the right. Sean stepped out waving his arms. Stan jolted to a halt, hoisted himself out with the use of the door frame. His body was twisted over to one side, almost as though he carried some form of deformity. Sean felt sorry for him but couldn't prevent a chuckle escaping from his lips.

"You've got it bad; you look as if you've shat yourself mate," said Sean.

Stan shook his head and opened the boot. "What you

THE PICTURE GAME

got?" he leant back. "Ooh yer bugger!"

"Six meds and three smalls," replied Sean, handing over the pictures.

Stan would usually double check them in, but tossed them in a basket. Sean reached up and closed the boot. Sue was already in the front seat; her face a picture of delight.

5
Top Seller Sue

"You done well," Sean said to Sue, shuffling in next to John.

"Yeah, six Big 'Uns, twelve meds, and fourteen smalls," she replied, clapping her hands in delight. Her upper body swayed as she performed her victory dance.

John shook his head with embarrassment, he'd had a bummer.

Sue reached over, poked Sean in the gut, "And what did you do?" she giggled.

Sean covered his face up with his hands, "Fuck off, I taught you too well, that's what I done."

"The first guy I sold to was a proper gentleman, he looked like Omar Sharif, he was lovely and wanted my phone number," she flicked her eyebrows.

"Hope you gave it to him, he just wanted to shag you," Sean said. "I think you found the Omar..."

Stan laughed, happy both Sean and John had had bummers, he winked at Sue, eased himself upright in his seat before pulling off.

Sean wondered if Stan was on one of his war wound stories as she leant over massaging his shoulders.

"Ahh, that's beautiful," said Stan, rolling his neck, "Oh, oh, yeah, yeah, that's good."

"Dirty old bastard," thought Sean. "He's laying it on thick."

"What price did you sell them at?" John said, glancing

THE PICTURE GAME

at Sean. "Tell Sean what you sold them at." Without giving her time to reply, he jumped in. "She got seventy quid for a set of four Big 'Uns, and forty quid for the other two. Gave them away," throwing his hands in the air.

Sue glanced over her shoulder, smiled sarcastically and blew him a kiss as she continued to massage Stan's shoulders. "I never sold them for that. I just told you I'd sold them for that, so you wouldn't get jealous." Grinning she added, "What did you sell again?" cupping her hand to her ear. "Sorry?"

"As per usual, the cunt's done fuck all!" Stan burst in laughing, looking up into his rear-view mirror.

Sue exploded with laughter.

"That's cheered you up, hasn't it, you twat," John sneered at Stan.

"Fucking right it has." Stan bellowed out. "Ooh, yer fucker," he jerked upright in pain.

Sue could not hold back the tears of laughter rolling down her face. John nudged Sean, leant over and began kneading his fingers into Stan's shoulders and neck.

"Fuck off! Fuck off!" Stan said, squealing in pain. "Fuck off you bastard, that hurts."

Some nights they would finish off the shift working pubs in the hope that alcohol would loosen purse strings, which it often did. Tonight, was such a night although John was the only one who wanted to work. It was a typical council estate pub, built in the sixties or seventies, large car-park and totally characterless. As was the routine, the seller went in first and was left to it. Each seller had their own blag and didn't need a 'helping hand', contradicting whatever was said.

Sue was gracious enough to buy the round. Stan and Sean sat in the furthest corner, next to a fruit machine. The bar was crowded with regulars, mostly middle aged men in shirts and jeans. John was talking to a tall slim man, who looked like a Status Quo fan in his leather waistcoat, jeans and white trainers; probably the landlord. They were stood

35

by the bar, when John showed him a picture, he'd pass it over the bar to a rosy-faced lady with dark wavy hair, probably the landlady. She divided the pictures into two piles, very quickly, and without any fuss. Occasionally she would show one back to leather waistcoat man, who'd either nod or shake his head, it then went on its relevant pile.

"Looks if he's doing alright," said Sean, taking a sip of lager. "Whatever pile they go for. How many has he done already?"

"He's only done four meds and a couple of smalls," Stan replied. Furtively he looked around the bar and took out a pack of tobacco and a rolling machine. He placed a small amount of the tobacco on the white cigarette paper, reaching for his denim jacket, he pulled out a small bag of weed and sprinkled some into his joint.

Sue was over at the pool table, playing with one of the regulars, a chubby bloke with a bald head.

Stan raised the roll-up to his lips and lit it, taking a long drag. "I'll feel a lot better after this."

He took a few more, before passing it over to Sean.

"That Sue's, proper gorgeous, ain't she," said Stan. Picking up a beer mat he scraped the spilt beer from the table. "Did you ever see Jackie Hall? She looks just like Sue," he looked over as Sue was taking a shot. "Same face same arse, but she didn't have Sue's tits.

Sean leant back, drawing deeply on the spliff.

John wandered over, he'd sold another six meds and two smalls, making it a reasonable night. He sat for a while with Sean and Stan before joining Sue at the pool table.

"Yeah, that Jackie used to work for Sully; you must have met her, almost the double of her," said Stan, nodding in Sue's direction. "I used to fuck her every night after the shift. I'd drop all the lads off then shag her in the back of the car."

Sean took another quick drag, before passing the joint

under the table to Stan. He had heard of the name Jackie Hall but didn't really know her. But not wanting to pour water on Stan's story, he let him go on.

Stan laughed, "Her husband found out. Fucking hell, the shit hit the fan. He tried to kill me the bastard." Taking a gulp of beer, he went on. "He turned up at my house on a Friday night with a gun, was gonna fucking shoot me. Yeah!" he nodded. "My missus and the babbies were in bed. I'm sitting with a couple of cans watching Starsky and Hutch when there's this almighty fucking bang on the door." He took another gulp and a drag on the spliff. "I shat myself, absolutely shat myself, thought the door was gonna come in. You know me," he paused waiting for Sean. "I'm not that fucking stupid, so I nipped upstairs, get my bat, I didn't know then, he had a gun. The wife's up out of bed, she's shitting herself, the kids are still sound asleep." Stan laughed at that, then lowered his voice to a whisper. "I get up to the window and peek out. I can see her old man, straight away he spots me, and starts shouting up at the window. Fucking Watkins, get out here, you arsehole." Stan waved his hands, as he acted out the scene. "Ranting and raving, he's going fucking crazy, waving this gun in the air, like fucking Buffalo Bill. Well I weren't going out to get me head blown off, so I drop my draws and squash my shitty arse against the window, and that's when the bastard shouts. And you too Sean Finn!" Stan laughed, slapped Sean on his back, repeating. "And you Sean Finn!"

6
Sully's Party Pub

John thumped his yellow wreck of a Ford Capri up on the pavement. "This place is a fucking dive." He eyed up the frontage. "I dunno why he is drinking in a shithole?"

"The beer's cheap," said Sean.

"Should be by the look of it," John replied, as he peeked through the stain glass windows. "Fucking hell, it's full of old boys again, there ain't gonna be any women in here." Dejected; his head dropped towards his chest.

"It will be alright, it's only one night," said Cormac, putting an arm around his old friend's shoulder.

"Fucking dump. Twat, I knew I shouldn't of bothered." replied John.

The pub door swung open, and out stepped Veronica with Sue. Veronica was wearing black boots and a cat-suit, she looked fantastic. Sue looked good too, she was wearing skin-tight jeans, and a fitted T-Shirt. Although Sue was very pretty, all eyes were on Veronica.

Sue rushed forward planting a kiss on Sean's lips.

"Is he in there?" Cormac asked, referring to Sully.

"Yeah, he's in there, half pissed. We're off," she replied.

"Where to?" John asked, his mood had lightened. "Stay for a drink," he pleaded.

Sue looked to Veronica, not wanting to disappoint her new friend but wanting to be with Sean.

Veronica shrugged, as if to say do what you like.

THE PICTURE GAME

"No, we're off," Sue said, playing hard to get, not realising Sean's interest was now only peripheral.

"Are you not going to the party?" asked Cormac, concerned Sully was rat arsed and there was no woman now to censor him.

"Later yeah, but Leamington first," Veronica replied. "We'll get back later." Veronica smiled over Cormac's shoulder at Sean, fixing her eyes on his. "You gonna be here?"

Sean was fond of Sue and didn't want to lose her, but now felt sure Veronica was interested. "Should be…" He was trying to be cool and breezy, but his mind was blank. Veronica held her gaze, embarrassed Sean lowered his eyes, intimidated by her boldness.

Sue caught the look, that 'later,' look. Feeling very much the bridesmaid and suddenly sober, she said, "It's almost eight, we're going to have to go."

Veronica smiled beguilingly, "We're already late, we're gonna have to love you and leave you boys," as she took Sue's arm.

They watched as the girls sashayed down the road, Sean hoping for a look back but neither girl did.

Cormac opened the pub door.

"He's a jammy bastard that Sully," said John.

Inside it was quiet and looked like more or less the same crowd from lunchtime, probably on the same drinks too. The barman raised an eye but continued a half-hearted conversation with the pock marked crossword man. Sitting facing the bar on a stool on his own was a scarlet faced old boy in a tweed hat. His face lit up with a broad smile as the boys entered, eyes following them as they looked around.

John whispered, "This is shit."

Sean laughed and nodded.

The elderly man raised his glass.

Sean responded, "How you doing?"

"Fair to middling." He replied, going on, "I'll be better after a few more of these." His voice wheezed as he spoke.

39

Cormac, glanced back, and asked, "Has this place got a bar?"

Disappointment marked the old boys face at the possibility of a conversation lost. Raising a hooked finger, he pointed towards the door at the other end of the lounge. "Good luck," he called, raising his glass.

"You can come if you like," Cormac called back, grinning.

The old boy raised himself a few inches from his seat as if to follow, straightened his tie, but with a wave sat back down. "You boys have a good night. I'll catch up with you later." Adding with a wink, "But if there's four of them, I'm your man."

Sean stuck up a thumb as they left the lounge.

The old boy glanced at the blank faces surrounding him, his day's mischief long since gone. Then catching the barman's eye, wheezed out. "Make it a double Frank."

They walked through a grimy passageway, that stank of piss. On entering the bar, the smell of stale beer and sweat hit them. Smoke clouded the ceiling, the music was loud, voices coarse and rowdy. A dark-haired lady sat by the bar was using two beer mats as a fan to cool herself. The barman was the opposite of the one in the lounge. Sweat dripping from his brow as he manically rushed to serve his customers.

Sully was standing side-on, his face glistening with a pearlescent sheen, pint in hand. He was talking to a guy immaculately dressed in a light grey flannel suit and tie, a handkerchief dangling from his top pocket, not a drop of sweat on him, nor a hair out of place. Leroy was sitting playing dominoes with two black older guys, both in baseball caps, and a whippet faced white man, all with sweat marks on their shirts.

Leroy looked up smiling at seeing John and shouted across the din, "You made it, I don't believe it!" A domino crashed to the table; one of the black guys nudged Leroy, it was his turn.

Sully had not noticed them as he was deep in conversation with his friend leaning against the bar.

Cormac had volunteered to get the round in and squashed in behind a red-haired fat man in a green vest, freckles and red hair on his shoulder. An opening appeared, he wedged himself alongside Sully, giving his friend a tap on the shoulder. Sully shuffled slightly to one side. Cormac jabbed him twice with a stiff thumb to the ribs.

Sully did not respond other than lean back, pressing his weight on Cormac. Then slowly, he peered over his shoulder, stern and challenging, but on recognising Cormac.

"Cormac!" Sully's face lit up with a crazy grin. "Bloody hell, I was going to belt you," he looked half cut, eye lids greasy and half-closed. He threw an arm over Cormac's shoulder, who wondered if his friend would last the night.

"Sean and John are over there," Cormac shouted in Sully's ear. He pointed a thumb over his shoulder. Puzzled, Sully leant closer, Cormac knew he was wasting his time.

"Billy this is Cormac," Sully shouted, then turning to Cormac, "Billy's up from London, he's up for the party."

Billy attempted to shake hands, but as he did so the man in the green vest barged between the two.

"I'll get them in," shouted Sully and waved confidently at the sweaty barman.

"Thank god for that", thought Cormac who did not fancy his chances of getting served.

Billy was looking intently at Cormac.

Cormac asked, "Have you known Sully for long?

Billy shook his head "Not that long." His face was extremely pale, his expression was passive and direct. He had steely blue eyes and without doubt he was wearing mascara, his long hair was tucked into the back of his collar.

THE PICTURE GAME

Such eccentricity Cormac was yet to encounter.

From his pocket, Billy took out a silver case. "How long have you known him?" He asked, his voice barely a whisper.

Cormac leant closer, "A fair old while. I make up pictures, I got to know him through that."

Billy opened the case which contained long black cigarettes, without offering Cormac one, he placed one in his mouth, closed the case and slipped it back into his pocket. He lit it with a jewel studded lighter.

Embarrassed, Cormac turned putting his hand on Sully's shoulder. The barman placed the complete order on the bar, and Sully passed them through. The guy in the green vest looked annoyed, mumbling as he was forced to retreat.

"Get out the fucking way Pete," said Sully.

Pete smiled and laughed on recognising Sully and moved to allow them through.

As they were making their way from the bar, Cormac asked, "Who's that guy," pointing in the direction of Billy.

"That fat fuck, he's alright, Pete Walker, he's an undertaker, got his own business," said Sully, mistakenly and then went on, "He's a decent guy, you'd like him." He handed over beers to Sean and John and then raised his. "Cheers for coming over lads."

Sean shouted, "What time's the party, are all this lot coming?"

"Most of them, yeah," said Sully. "Locals, I hardly know them, but fuck it." With a wicked smile Sully directed his eyes towards two awkward-looking middle aged men, talking to two young women.

One of the guys was much taller than the other with a Jason King style moustache. He was cracking jokes, clearly more amused than his audience. The shorter one, bald apart from a horseshoe of dark hair was wearing a light blue suit, one hand in his pocket, the other holding his drink.

42

Sully nodded at the girls, "That's Marie, the skinny one is Gloria."

Marie was an attractive brunette, dressed in a short black leather skirt with a studded belt which sat low on her hips, she wore a pink top, black stilettos completed her look. The taller of the men tentatively brushed his hand over Maria's hips, she whispered in his ear. Raising an eyebrow, he turned to say something to his friend. Baldy looked shocked, then grinned, a wide lecherous grin, not quite your Shakespeare's Lothario, more your Sid James.

The boys laughed.

"Dirty bastards," said Cormac.

Sully leant in even closer; his eyes had changed from a dull stare to bright alertness. "Marie's one of those girls, just loves the dick. Gloria's her mate, don't really know too much about her."

Gloria looked soulless, her blond hair was thick and wavy, with thin painted lips she puffed on a cigarette. She was flat-chested with hip bones that jutted over the top of a white mini skirt. She smiled at the short bald man, then the taller before blankly gazing around the room.

Sully straightened up in disgust. "I wouldn't mind but they asked to come over." He shook his head, "She ain't gonna earn fuck all with a face like a smacked arse, fucking miserable-looking cow."

The boys once again fell about laughing. John spitting a mouth full of beer across the room.

"I don't blame her, who'd wanna shag one of them old bastards," said Cormac.

"She looks horny, in a bored secretary way," said John.

"Na' too skinny, pretty face mind," Sean replied. "I wouldn't mind getting hold of Maria though."

"Twenty five quid and it can be arranged," Sully winked.

Cormac glanced back to the bar; Pete Walker had cornered Billy in a conversation. Billy looked up catching Cormac's eye and smiled, Cormac turned away.

THE PICTURE GAME

7
Sully's House Party

It was late but still warm outside when they left the pub. Sully, along with Leroy and Murphy, had gone ahead to set up. Cormac, Sean and John had chipped in and bought a few can from the off-licence on the way. They turned into Sully's road, a uniform row of Victorian terrace houses, front doors directly onto the street. A reggae beat vibrated up the street to meet them. As they approached Sully's house, an old banger pulled up outside. A bare-chested man got out, shouting angrily back at his companions. He was followed a fat lad who staggered after the first guy, bouncing off the door frame as he entered the house. Two girls, emerged from the back seats, giggling with laugher.

One shouted, "Fuck off you twats."

John called out, "Sally."

She turned, "John, John, where've you been?"

John kissed her on the cheek. "What's up with Steve, where's his shirt gone?"

Sally grimaced as she held on to John, both swaying back and forth to stay on their feet. "He lost it in a fight. You know what he's like." She flung her arms in the air, giggling. "Arsehole!"

Suddenly her stiletto heel buckled taking them both tumbling to the ground. With a bit of heaving they were pulled back to their feet. Unaware to Sally, one of her tits had popped out over her dress.

THE PICTURE GAME

Her girlfriend tried to cover Sally's bare tit, saying, "Cover yourself up you tart; your tits are showing."

"What you doing, get off me," said Sally, pushing her friend away. Then realizing she was exposed, "Bloody hell, that's you, John Kelly, grabbing me."

"Come on, you daft tart," said John, as he took her by the arm.

Sally giggled, "Lead on McDuff," they linked together and stumbled on towards Sully's.

As with the pub the place was heaving and heat stifling. Dillinger's *'I got cocaine in my brain'* hummed off the walls, the bass like a soft thump to the head. Murphy lowered his head and raised a hand, acknowledging the boys, and took another draw of his spliff. He looked sharp in a Jimi Hendrix T-shirt, mirror sunglasses and a porkpie hat. He was dancing a slow grind behind the decks and towards the end of the record, slid the volume down, MC-ing over the record.

"Hey Jim, Jim, just a minute y'all
I want to ask you somethin'
I want you to spell somethin' for me Jim
Can you do that? Sure John But I want you to spell for me, New York!"

The party sang back, to Murphy's orchestration.

"A knife, a fork, a bottle and a cork
That's the way we spell New York
Right on, out of sight man, right on, ooh
Right on, yeah, right on..."

The room was about fifteen-foot square and was empty apart from Murphy's sound system. One wall was decorated with a pencil sketch of Bob Marley surrounded by lions and beautiful naked girls. On another a poster of a naked man, his body and face contorted, as if frozen in a

THE PICTURE GAME

giant ice cube. The back wall was filled with a massive antique gilt mirror, the glass warped, distorting the reflection, giving an effect of a seedy nightclub frequented by dwarfs and hobgoblins.

The floorboards creaked to Murphy's beat, by his side was a stack of records, which he sifted through, shuffling and reshuffling, repeatedly.

In the kitchen, Leroy had set up a bar. If you hadn't bought your own, you could buy a can of red stripe or a shot of whisky, rum or vodka, everything a pound.

Sally and her friend danced back and forth in front of the decks. She'd moved provocatively close to Murphy, her hips swishing like a lioness's tail for attention. Murphy passed her his spliff over the decks. She took a long draw then handed it to her friend who without taking a toke, passed it back. Dennis Brown's, *Money in my Pocket*, played with Murphy easing up behind Sally, his crotch in rhythm with her gyrations. Steve her boyfriend glared from the back of the room. Cormac was drinking whisky, watching the room, Sean and John were in the kitchen talking to Leroy.

Murphy looked up, from the corner of his eye he could see Sully who had taken over the decks, he had hold of an album, *Sticky Fingers*, by the Rolling Stones and was hovering. poised like a drunken cobra, unsure when to strike. Sully stumbled, there was a horrible scratching noise. Murphy winced, getting back to his station before Sully could do any more damage, Sally not realising he was gone was left gyrating to an invisible partner. There was a bit of pushing and shoving as they fought for control of the turntable with Sully playfully barging Murphy away, Murphy cursed, Sully took no notice, waving him away with a drunken sweep of his arm.

The crowd watched as Sully focused and gently placed the needle on the record. The song did not play, Sully grinned and raised his arms. A second later, the unmistakable opening notes of The Rolling Stones' *Brown*

Sugar thundered out from the speakers. He played with the volume, blasting it up and down, then up again. Cormac smiled as he sipped on his whiskey watching Sully pull a group in a drunken huddle around the room. Others joined in with the unruly sways, with the stumbling turning into a conga, Sully out in front.

"Brown Sugar how come you dance so good" they whooped and hollered.

Leroy had joined on at the back, which gave Cormac a thought, wondering if his bar might be unmanned. Quickly he downed his drink and headed to the kitchen, on his way stepping over a couple sitting crossed legged, blankly staring at each other, as the conga moved upstairs. In the kitchen a group of men from the pub were arguing about the Falklands war.

"For fuck's sake, who gives a fuck?" thought Cormac.

A guy in a denim jacket was talking to Marie, '*Brown Sugar,* ' she shouted, leaving the man to himself as she joined the end of the line.

A skinny older black guy in a snappy blue pinstriped suit was helping himself to a generous glass of Johnny Walker. His face was thin with hollow cheeks, moist yellow eyes displayed his roguish intent. Spotting Cormac a broad grin spread across his face, he glanced around furtively as he raised his glass to his lips.

"My man Cormac," he said, grabbing Cormac's hand firmly.

It was Cecil, Leroy's uncle. Cormac shook his empty tumbler. Cecil took a quick swig of his own, refilling it before filling Cormac's.

"While the cat's away," he said, in a strong Jamaican accent, followed by a joyous cackle.

"You should have heard me just around midnight," blasted from the front room.

Cormac raised his glass.

"How are you doing, my man?" Cecil asked.

Before Cormac could answer, Cecil grimaced. "Quick."

THE PICTURE GAME

They downed their drinks as Sully led the conga through, Leroy peeled off and poured himself a rum.

"Leroy how you supposed to get a drink around here when the barman off dancing around the fucking room." Cormac thrust his glass forward, "Come on man, one for me and one for my man Cecil."

Cecil placed his empty glass on the makeshift bar, rubbing his hands together.

Leroy raised the bottle of Johnny Walker, "Someone's been at this bottle, look there's the mark," he glared accusingly at both.

"I've been here all the time man, no one's been near that bottle," Cecil said, ham acting, his face curled in distain. "Cormac's just come in now, dis' second before you," he said indignantly. "You come back from dancing like a fool and start accusing people of stealing drink man. You take your bottles with you next time, t'clown."

Cecil's bluster had worked, Leroy meekly poured and handed over the drinks.

"Who's that?" asked Cormac.

Leroy looked up; Billy was smoking one of his long black cigarettes in the hallway. "I don't know. A mate of Sull's I think, he looks queer. Definitely an arsehole with that daft fag in his mouth." He turned to Cormac. "You owe me two quid."

Cormac divvied up.

Billy had moved closer.

As he did so, Cecil leant to one side to get a better look. "He's evil man," he whispered to Cormac. "Look, his eyes, a devil," he added with surprise, "He got make-up on," adding, "Batty boy!" with a look of disgust. "Keep away from that man, I'll tell you he's a devil. See his eyes, see they don't register nothing, noth'ting. When I look at him, I fixed him, but noth'ting, dead man, dead." He took another swig of whiskey, tipped his glass under the bottle.

Leroy reluctantly obliged.

Cecil turned once more to Cormac, "Deadman, I tell

you."

A scream rang out from the front room followed by shouts. Steve, Sally's boyfriend, stumbled into the kitchen holding his face, bright red blood oozing through his fingers. Close on his heels was Sully, who hit him with the heel of a bottle. Steve dropped to the floor in front of Cormac.

"Hey fucking hell Sully!" Cormac said trying to get between the two.

Sully didn't answer but barged Cormac to one side, he grabbed hold of Steve pulling him by the hair across the floor into the hallway. "Get that fucker out of here," he screamed. Sully lost his grip as a clump of Steve's hair came out in his hand, he then began stamping on his stricken foe.

"Sully, Sully, for fuck's sake, he's had enough," said Leroy intervening.

Sully loomed over Steve, "Get him out, I want that fucker out of here." He screamed, "Wanker, wanker!" Thumping him on the side of his face with every expletive.

Leroy was now between the two and picked Steve up by his arm. It was obvious that his nose had been broken as it was all over to one side. John lifted his other arm and between them, they helped him to the door.

"I'm all right," Steve said belligerently. "Tell that slut she can fuck off. Nigger meat," he shouted.

"You don't make it easy on yourself, do you mate?" Leroy said, slinging him out the door.

Sully followed, and before Leroy had time to stop him, he booted Steve in the head.

"Leave him, you'll kill him," said Leroy, holding Sully back.

Steve tried to get up but slumped falling in a heap. John dragged him over to the side, propping him on his arse against a wall. "Are you alright mate?" he asked.

Dazed, Steve nodded, "I'm alright."

Steve's mate appeared and with the help of John they

THE PICTURE GAME

lifted him to his feet, lying him into the rear seats of his car.

"You need to get him to the hospital, get him checked out," said John

"I will," said Steve's mate, getting in the driver's seat. He started up the car, the crowd dispersed as it turned the corner.

Like a pack of jackals, a group had congregated around their king, feeding off the blood and violence. Sully himself didn't take too much notice of the cheers and backslaps. He seemed nervous as he picked up a fresh bottle of beer, downing it in one.

Sally was in floods of tears as she left to find her man, John followed in the hope she didn't.

Sean, was picking up shards of glass off the floor, he glanced up at his brother.

Cormac bent down beside him and picked a few slithers. "What happened?" he asked.

Sean looked nervous and spoke in a whisper. "It was Murphy, he was fucking about with Steve's missus. Steve grabbed her and slaps her. Sully went fucking berserk, booted the cunt from here to fucking kingdom come."

"Did he hit him with a glass?" Cormac asked.

"Nah, he hit him with the end of the bottle, glasses just got knocked over," said Sean.

"His face looked a mess," Cormac replied.

"He shit himself as soon as he saw it was Sully, he was trying to back off, didn't even try to throw a punch," said Sean, shaking his head.

"He's is a fucking animal," Cormac glanced over at Sully. Putting his hand on his brother's shoulder, "You ok?"

"Yeah, I'm alright," Sean said but didn't look it, his eyes were wide and frightened.

Cormac leant in, "If that fucker ever lays a finger on you, I'll kill the bastard," he held Sean's head, looking him square in the eye.

THE PICTURE GAME

"I mean it."

8
The Drive Home with Billy

Sully was rolling a spliff later as Cormac approached. "Hey man, I'm really sorry about that arsehole earlier. I didn't invite him. I don't know the fuck, Sally's bloke, completely out of order."

"Fair enough," said Cormac warily.

She's a great girl, he must be one of the jealous types," Sully laughed. "He'll have to sort himself out."

As he was talking, Billy approached, his smile wide and friendly. "Can I get you guys a drink?"

"Yeah, you want a Red Stripe," Sully asked.

"Red Stripe and whiskey?" Cormac replied."

Billy wandered off.

Cormac nudged Sully, "What's with him it with the hair business?"

Before Sully could answer, he was distracted, as into the room stepped Veronica, along with Sue. His eyes lit upon seeing her. "Hiya sweetheart, you managed to get back."

Veronica planting a kiss full on Sully's lips. "Mmmm."

Sue threw her arms around Sean, they embraced and kissed, and whilst they did, Sean's eyes strayed to Veronica.

"What do you want to drink babe?" Sully asked.

"Billy's getting them in," Veronica responded. She looked around the room at the broken glass. "What have I missed?"

THE PICTURE GAME

"Ah nothing, some wanker took a swing at Sally, so I fucked him out," Sully said boastfully.

"You been fighting again?" her eyes were bright, alert with excitement.

"Nothing I'll tell you later." Sully was playing the strong silent type.

"How'd it go in Leamington?" Cormac asked.

Veronica smiled, "Really good, they wanted us to stay, but I wouldn't miss my man's party."

Billy laughed as he returned, loaded up with a bottle of Champagne and a stack of glasses, which he passed around. "Don't worry gents I haven't forgotten you," pulling cans of beer from his pockets. He unwrapped the wire and foil cover of the champagne bottle and popped the cork, "But first Champagne." He filled the glasses. "I know it's a bit late, but I thought it best to wait for the ladies. Happy Birthday mate," he raised his glass.

The toast was made to cheers from everyone.

A few shook up beer cans, soaking Sully.

"Happy Birthday Sully," they cheered, with beer spraying around the room. Some made a feeble attempt to give Sully the bumps, but it was half-hearted, they didn't even get him off his feet.

Sully glanced up just as Veronica's eyes flicked to Sean.

Relax, by Frankie Goes to Hollywood came on, Sully, Veronica, together with Sue and Sean took to the dancefloor.

Billy took Cormac to one side to talk. It was apparent he was not the weird silent cobra he had appeared earlier in the evening. Instead he was very much a raconteur, with stories of his early life in Somerset where he lived with his family on a stud farm. He talked mostly about his father, an accomplished jockey who had died far too young from lung cancer, Cormac could see as Billy talked the death of his father still affected him. His business was investments which took him all over the world, staying in exotic locations for months of the year. The stories told were exciting and glamorous, only embellished with a light polish.

Billy asked Cormac about his own family. Cormac seemed embarrassed and reluctant to say much, maybe it was because next to Billy his life seemed so ordinary.

Billy sensed this and stopped him.

"Never be ashamed of who you are, be true to yourself," but curiously added, "We are out of people's lives sooner than we think."

Sean approached and swung an arm over his Cormac's shoulder, Sue slung her arm over his other. They were joined by Veronica and Sully.

Veronica pulled out a small bag of speed, "A little pick me up, anyone?"

With Sean by his side Cormac plucked up courage and asked Billy why he wore make-up and his hair inside his collar. Billy explained, it was a habit he got into, no real reason. Seeing the boys smiling, he admitted that perhaps it was strange, but went on to say that it also picked him out, people remembered him. He suggested that they too should adopt an eccentricity. Maybe earrings for Cormac and eyeshadow for Sean.

They both laughed, saying "No way," although Sean wondered maybe once Veronica said it was a good idea.

The party limped on, empty beer bottles, cans, and glasses littered every room. Gloria was slumped in a chair with Murphy, he'd made his money, with enough manic-eyed people wandering around to prove it. Cecil had taken charge of the record collection playing some old-time sweet soul music, nursing the party through to daylight. Sully and Veronica were smooching to the Supremes on the dance floor.

Billy said he was leaving and offered to drop off Cormac and Sean. Cormac said it would be great if he could drop them at the station. But Billy insisted he would drop them home, saying he had to call in and see a friend

THE PICTURE GAME

in Birmingham anyway. Cormac gave his brother a sharp nudge, Sean wasn't ready to go, he was sitting with Sue, her head on his lap as he watched Sully and Veronica out of one eye. He winked across to his brother, saying he'd catch up the following day.

Billy drove a 1962 Porsche 356, which he said he'd won it in a bet, it looked sleek and sexy. Cormac didn't have a clue what a 356 was, so Billy explained the history of Porsche, which in a sober state Cormac would have enjoyed but it went over his head.

It was strange sitting so low. Cormac joked that his trolley as a kid was higher off the ground.

Billy laughed, saying "Yeah, but you won't get your dick sucked whilst sitting on your trolley."

"That's not what Mary O'Brien thought," chipped Cormac back.

They drove straight through the centre of Stratford. Cormac was fearful that they may get stopped and advised a different route, but Billy was unconcerned.

"Have you boys always lived in Coventry?" Billy asked, lighting up one of his cigarettes.

"Yeah," Cormac replied. Realising his speech was slurred; he wound down the window sucking in a few lung fulls of fresh air. "Dublin," he blurted.

"What you're from Dublin? Billy glanced back, a bit confused.

Cormac nodded, "Mum is."

"What part of Dublin?"

"Rathgar."

Things went silent for a while.

"So how long have you been selling pictures?" Billy asked, as he glanced up at his rear-view mirror.

Cormac answered guardedly, "A few years, I don't do any selling myself but have got teams that go out, I run the business."

Billy looked suitably impressed.

Cormac went on, "I don't want to deal that much with

sellers, most of them are idiots. Wanted to get a few more teams but..., I don't know?"

"Any business you need people you can rely on. How do the teams recruit sellers?" asked Billy.

Cormac laughed, "Fuck knows, any fucker who turns up."

Billy laughed, shaking his head.

Cormac wound the window closed, "I'd wanna get in professional people, not these arseholes, most of em' can earn a couple of hundred quid in a night and they'll still be scrounging for their breakfast in the morning." He went on, "If I can get organised, maybe it would take a year or so, I reckon I could be the biggest in the city." As the words left him, he thought how stupid it sounded. His head was humming, he wound the window back down, breathing in gulps of air, trying to pick up on landmarks as they passed.

Billy looked over, "You okay?"

"Yeah, I'm fine."

Billy placed his hand on Cormac's knee, "Do you want to stop, get out for a while?"

The touch of Billy's hand on his knee startled Cormac, it felt good but also made him uneasy. Billy's hand lingered and began to creep up his thigh. Cormac was caught between fear and longing.

Billy studied Cormac for a brief moment, then lifted his hand back to the steering wheel. He smiled, "What you need is a plan, with a deadline for recruiting. Maybe set it up so the sellers buy the picture, or you could up their commission, that way you'll get the right people who really want to work, but fuck em off quick if they're shit." He pushed open a tiny window to flick out his ash. "From what I understand, it's a bit of a social club, work one day, piss up the next." Adding, "Saying that, it could be worse."

Cormac glanced over, although the touch was only fleeting, it excited him, was Billy coming on to him?

THE PICTURE GAME

"Yeah, you're right," He replied having not listened as the trees flashed by in a blur.

Billy continued, "No, I think you'll be ok; you've got your head screwed on, maybe need to chill out a bit more," he winked and grinned. Leaning forward on the steering wheel, he twisted his neck from side to side as if releasing a strain. "Sully's alright, but most of those lads there this evening I wouldn't trust with my granny's pension. Work only with people you trust."

"The only ones I'd trust are Sean and maybe John," said Cormac. "John's a good mate, I've known him for years," he stuttered, "They're the only two guys," his mind still spinning.

"Billy glanced over and nodded in agreement. "You're a good lad, Cormac."

They arrived at Cormac's house, it was a quarter to six, with the dawn chorus accentuated by the stillness of the morning. Cormac thanked Billy for the lift home and waved as he pulled off.

Twenty yards up the road the car stopped and reversed. Billy wound down the window. "Listen, I was just thinking, I'm planning a party at my house, it would be great if you guys could make it," adding, "Free booze, I throw one every now and again, gets people together, good for business. You can't go wrong, free food and free booze, you'll have a great time."

Cormac thought for a moment, grinned, "Yeah, I'd love to."

"O.K, give me your address so I can get a proper invitation off. What about your brother?" asked Billy.

"He'd love it."

Billy opened the glove compartment and took out a leather-bound notebook and gold pen. Cormac scribbled down his address. At the top of the page he wrote Cormac and Sean Finn and handed it back

Billy looked at the names, "The Deadly Finns," he smiled.

THE PICTURE GAME

9
Billy's Party

Three weeks later a cream watermarked envelope dropped through the letterbox. Ma picked it up off the doormat wondering what was in the fancy looking letter, she flipped it over, looking at it up at the light. "Probably from the bank," she thought and placed it prominently next to the clock and the sacred heart picture.

Cormac spotted the it as soon as he got home and knowing exactly what it was, rushed to open it. The invitation card had a picture on the front, Pop art, brightly coloured, showing a bull and a crocodile in a carnal embrace. The crocodile had wrapped its tail around the loins of the bull, whilst the bull's member had slipped between the crocodile's hindquarters. Cormac felt embarrassed with his mother looking over his shoulder. It read:

William Fox requests the pleasure of
Cormac Finn esquire and Sean Finn esquire
To an Evening Drinks Soirée
21st June 1981
Drinks served at 7.00pm
R.S.V.P.
Denmark House,
Plymouth Street, Kensington.
London.

THE PICTURE GAME

His face beamed, reading it repeatedly.

"Are you's going to a party in London," Ma asked, as she tried to pinch the card from Cormac's fingers.

"Ah, ah, it's not yours," Cormac said, "It's for me and Sean, a friend of ours is having a party."

Ma was not put off, and quickly snatched the card, "You'll not be having secrets from your Mother."

Turning, she fended his attempts to grab it back, glancing at the picture quickly as she opened it up the invitation. "Now, aren't you the two dandies, off to London for a party. Esquires eh!" she nodded approvingly. She returned to the picture on the front, examining it closely, her face appeared puzzled, then disgusted. "What in God's name is that buffalo doing to the crocodile?" Moving the card back and forth, she focused, "Jesus! It looks as if it's trying to wang the arse of it." She shook her head disapprovingly, handing it back. "Dirty, dirty, dirty." adding "God Almighty, what's the world coming to." Looking her son in the eye, "I hope it's not monkey business at this party."

Cormac grabbed the card back and shot upstairs. Sitting on the edge of the bed, he studied it for a while, not quite sure what to make of the picture himself.

Later, when Sean arrived, Cormac showed him, Sean's expression was much like his mother's. "Fucking Hell, that's weird," he said.

The weeks went by without incident, the 21st of June arrived, Sully was due to pick them up at 3.30pm.

Ma had checked over their rented dinner suits again and again and taken their photographs, first singularly, then together and after a bit of fuss setting up the camera timer, with Ma in the middle.

At 4pm a car horn sounded.

Somehow Sully had managed to get hold of a brand-new Jag', deep maroon in colour, with Veronica sitting next to him, they looked the part.

Ma called out, "Fill-em stars, yous look just like fil'm

61

THE PICTURE GAME

stars." She had them line up, the two boys stood either side of the car, with Veronica and Sully eased up on to the bonnet, Ma took a few more snaps. Veronica wore a long satin black dress, which fanned out at the bottom. Sully's suit was tailored to perfection, white cuffs with silver and black cufflinks, his bow tie hung loosely around his neck. Neither Cormac nor Sean matched the elegance of the couple, but nonetheless cut a figure.

Photos taken, Veronica offered the front seat to Cormac the tallest of the group and jumped into the back with Sean. The car had a drinks cabinet, which Sully had stocked up for the journey. Those were the days when drinking and driving were not exclusive so as Cormac and Sully sipped beer, Veronica and Sean started a bottle of whisky. The weather was gloomy as they left Coventry, but by the time, they hit the M1, it had cleared up enough to open the sunroof.

Veronica and Sean chatted about music, Sean said he was planning to start a band and had taught himself to play a couple of Bob Dylan and Neil Young tunes. Cormac who was earwigging peered over his shoulder smiling knowing this was bullshit. Veronica said she loved Neil Young, and asked if she could call over to hear him play. With the sound of the wind racing through the car Sean leant in close to hear, he could feel her lips gently brush the edge of his ear. Sully looked up from his driving, asking what they were whispering about?

"You," Veronica said laughing. "I'm telling Sean what a miserable bastard you are."

As Sully looked away, she gave Sean a crafty wink.

"She's crazy Sean, don't believe a word she says," said Sully.

"Am I now?" Veronica replied, "I didn't realise you boys were that close, all boys together is it? Well you can't have Sean, I'm gonna take him home with me!" with a giggle, she pulled Sean's arm through hers.

"You're welcome to her mate, but don't say I didn't

THE PICTURE GAME

warn you. She'll chew you up and after she's finished, she'll spit you out." Sully laughed.

Veronica leant in planting a sloppy wet kiss on Sean's cheek. "He's mine."

Sean knew he was being played with but didn't mind. Sully smiled sympathetically from the rear-view mirror.

They arrived in London for about 5pm.

Sully spoke, "Hey, we better get something to eat, Billy's food will be dodgy, crabs, lobsters, fishy shit."

They stopped at The Elegant Chicken, five minutes off the M1, a typical cafe they used often when working. A red frontage, with a sign above the door with a smiling chicken in a dinner suit. It was usually pretty empty, today was no different. Two blond ladies sat chatting over a coffee by the window, they were wearing matching striped blue T-shirts and white pedal pushers and could have been twins, apart from one being twice the size of the other. The Cafe owner, Mr Papadopoulos was short, five foot six or seven, pock marked skin, thick grey hair and a nine o'clock shadow. He glanced up as they entered.

The largest of the ladies looked around at the newcomers, with a snigger. "Bloody James Bond convention."

After a minute or so of deciding what to order, Sully and Cormac chose the all-day breakfasts. Sean went for shepherd's pie, Veronica said she wasn't hungry, then changed her mind and ordered an all-day breakfast too. The boys made short work of their meals whereas Veronica barely nibbled hers, in fact, it would be a push to say she started. Sitting for a while letting their food digest, they lit up a cigarette or two before leaving. It was still early, so they headed to a pub for a couple of pints. At seven-thirty they made their way to the party.

Billy's road was wide and expensive. They parked up and walked up the sweeping drive towards Denmark House. Sully and Veronica were in front, Cormac and Sean a few steps behind. Cormac checked his jacket for the invitation.

Sully stopped, "For fuck's sake, forgot to do up my dickie bow."

With the help of Veronica managed a passable knot, Sean and Cormac smiled; pinging their elasticated versions.

The house was regency style, double fronted with wide steps leading up to the front door. Gardens surrounded the front, with flower beds of rhododendron intermingled with smaller shrubs. Ornamental cherry trees were dotted throughout. A yew and laurel hedge provided a screen from the road.

Cormac held up his invitation but was totally ignored by the waiter in the doorway. Following Sully and Veronica's lead, Sean and Cormac helped themselves to a glass of champagne.

A huge crystal chandelier hung in the entrance hall, the ceilings were cavernous, the dominant colours were white and Duck Egg Blue. Guests were milling around, all in evening dress, some wore masquerade masks. They glanced around, there was no sign of Billy.

Feeling nervous, Cormac and Sean stuck close to Sully and Veronica. A stunningly beautiful woman passed by in a long flimsy white gown, accompanied by a grey-haired Asian man, with a very square face. She smiled at Sully, who nodded acknowledgement.

"Who's that?" a stunned Sean asked.

"Daughter of some rich banker bloke, you got no chance, unless you've got a spare million." He went on, "Billy knows the family well, Imelda, or Jemima something like that. The Paki is one of her dad's clients, he owns a load of car franchises, absolutely loaded, always with good-looking women."

Sully identified anyone he knew, giving away any secrets he had them. Like the young guy in the fox mask they passed on the way in, he was an Earl or something, somewhere up north, a backdoor bandit. Then there was the middle-aged lady, who looked like the queen, a smack head but a brilliant artist.

Sully pointed up the stairway to some gothic style paintings on the landing, "There's some of her work."

"What they go for?" asked Sean.

"Not sure of the big ones, but I know what Billy paid that small one," he pointed up to a piece, a man with a hares head, "ten grand. You wouldn't believe it, would you?"

"Bloody hell, ten grand. I bet Rolf don't even get that," Sean said, taking a closer look, "Did she paint the picture on the front of the invitation?

Sully responded, "Don't think so but maybe."

"Ten fucking grand, fucking hell, you'd buy a house for that in Cov," said Cormac in disbelieve.

Sully continued around the house. "Oh, you'll love it down here."

The basement was decorated with erotic paintings, pencil drawings, there was table tennis, a huge TV and in the middle a snooker table. Two young men with their jackets off were playing. One rosy-faced and plump, the other skinny, straight like his cue, neither seemed able to pot a ball.

Sully introduced the thin guy as Francis, who in turn introduced Rupert, his plump companion. Francis asked if they would care to join them for a game of doubles.

"Maybe later," Sully said. "We've just arrived. Do you know where Billy is?"

Francis said, "Yeah, he was upstairs a few minutes ago." As he talked to the group, something about Cormac caught his eye. "Later," he called as they wandered on, Cormac turned and smiled.

They wandered on through the crowds and after five minutes spotted Billy, unlike the rest of his guests in formal attire, he was wearing an Hawaiian shirt and linen trousers, he was giving instructions to a waiter.

"Fucking hell, I have been looking for you. I was

THE PICTURE GAME

beginning to wonder if you weren't coming," said Billy.

Cormac pushed to the front, "We've been here for about twenty minutes," the drink had given him confidence. "It's a great place you got here, it must have cost you a packet."

"I don't own, I rent it, two grand a month," Billy answered openly. "I've been here for three years now. It's a lovely place, I only wish I could afford to buy it. Most months I'm struggling to find the rent," he laughed.

Billy chatted to guests as they passed, taking over the tour from Sully. There were three other reception rooms downstairs, all filled with party-goers. He led them up through the house, stopping to point out a beautiful stained-glass window, a representation of George and the Dragon in a style not too dissimilar to the image on the front of their invitation.

Knocking on one of the bedroom doors, "Just in case," he joked.

The room was spacious and airy, painted white throughout, two huge windows stretched from floor to ceiling, the other bedrooms on the floor were similar. The bathrooms were Rococo in style, lots of gold. On the next floor were another three bedrooms, these were simpler in style, with a colonial feel. In one of the rooms a group of about ten very attractive teenagers had congregated, some were on the floor, others on couches, drinking and smoking.

There were also two girls who seemed older. One with spiky blonde hair, on recognising Sully, shouted over asking him why he didn't call her anymore.

"Because you always get me into trouble," Sully responded defensively.

The girl eyed up Veronica suspiciously holding her gaze for a while. Veronica glared back, curled her lip and kissed her teeth, letting out a click from the side of her mouth.

Billy frowned, raising his eyebrows as he talked to the

66

spiky haired girl, "Rose you are supposed to be looking after this lot, they'll have to come downstairs sooner or later."

There was a bit of loose banter between Sully and Rose as the rest looked on.

Before leaving Billy called out, "Come downstairs, mingle you sad bastards." He looked to Rose, "Bring them down."

A few shuffled to their feet and followed. Sully approached Veronica. "Honestly, Sweetheart, I didn't expect to see her."

Veronica hooked arms with Sean. "That's his ex-wife, she's a slut."

Sully glanced over at Cormac making a slashing sign with his finger across his neck. "In the shit again," he murmured.

Veronica overheard, and glared over her shoulder.

"Fucking women." Sully mumbled, from the side of his mouth.

Billy led them into the ballroom, where most people were gathered. Taking Cormac by the arm, he led him across to a stout gentleman, who looked out of place. Peter was by himself, dressed in tweeds with a glass of whiskey in hand.

"Cormac this is Peter O'Loughran or Big Peter, he's a horse trainer, and was a very good friend of my fathers." Billy placed an arm over one of Peters massive shoulders. "Peter this is Cormac Finn, he's from Coventry and runs a busy manufacturing operation, supplying artwork all over the country, doing very well for himself. But best of all he's a fellow Paddy, from Dublin."

Cormac had not heard his business described in this manner and felt a little embarrassed.

Big Peter's eyes lit up, "Ah, Dublin, I know it well," his broad Irish accent evident. "From Donegal myself, a beautiful little place called Dungloe, have you heard of it?" He stuck out his huge paw of a hand grabbing

THE PICTURE GAME

Cormac's, shaking it vigorously.

Before Cormac could respond, the thin young man, Francis, who had been playing snooker approached, sticking a sharp finger into Billy's ribs.

"Ah," said Billy turning, "you met Francis downstairs, didn't you Cormac? I don't know if you spoke?"

"Not really," answered Cormac shaking his head.

"Well, this is Francis, he's a cheeky little bastard, but I love him," said Billy. He hugged the thin young man, they both grinned. "Fortunately, he's a better jockey than snooker player."

Cormac forwarded his hand once more, and despite his size, Francis's grip was equally as hard as big Peter's. Francis' complexion was clear and pale, he had scars above both eyes, he looked more like a lightweight boxer than a jockey.

"Pleased to meet you." They said in unison.

Laughing, they smiled embarrassed at their harmony. Cormac proceeded to ask both Big Peter and Francis about the racing world, saying he enjoyed the odd flutter and was eager for any tips. Billy left the three of them talking and wander off with a Chinese lady who insisted he show her the gardens.

Anxious on his own Cormac glanced around for his brother or Sully who were nowhere to be seen.

Francis sensed Cormac's nervousness and led the conversation, asking about the pictures. He wanted to know how they were made up, areas chosen, commission, the whole operation. Normally paranoid about giving too much information away, Cormac had taken a liking to Francis and gave him the full lowdown, as a nonplussed Peter looked on.

"I'll leave you two lovebirds to it," Big Peter winked, heading off, empty glass in hand, in the direction of a waiter.

Cormac glanced up again looking for Sean.

Sean was now in the gardens with Veronica at his side,

68

THE PICTURE GAME

along with other guests who were enjoying the warmth of the evening. People were seated on benches and garden chairs; some had settled down on picnic rugs. Others were in bathing costumes standing around a grey stone swimming pool. The water was green and murky, you could barely see the legs of the bathers. Some who didn't have costumes were in their underwear.

Billy was remonstrating, with the Chinese lady giving him support, "It's bloody filthy, don't blame me if you all come down with typhoid. It's bloody filthy," he repeated shaking his head.

A man scooped up some water throwing it in Billy's direction who jumped back to avoid getting wet.

"Come on, get in, it's absolutely wonderful! We've swum in water a lot dirtier than this in India," said a slim dark-haired woman as she paddled on her back. "It's fine, get in." She too sent a splash of water in Billy's direction.

The Asian man who had been with Jemima or Imelda, earlier took a run and jump toward the woman. He grabbed at her, and both disappeared below the surface, a second or two they resurfaced.

"Bastard," she screamed and grabbing his head ducked him. He disappeared, she looked nervous, a second or two later, he re-emerged about two yards behind her.

"You need to be quicker Sophie." He spoke in refined English.

Sophie turned and darted after him, but he submerged like a dolphin. "Where are you, you bugger?" she scanned the surface and turned a full three-sixty degrees.

The Asian guy emerged once more, towards the end of the pool, Sophie scrambled after him, he was off again.

"Too slow," he called, and disappeared.

"Bloody lunatics, Nadir leave her alone," Billy called out.

"Looks like they're having fun," said Veronica, leading Sean up some steps between a laurel hedge which opened out into an orchard.

THE PICTURE GAME

Billy waved up, calling out, "Bloody Loonies, they'll all be sick!"

Sean and Veronica waved back and sat themselves on a bench next to a stone planter with pink lilies. Sean snapped off a single stem and presented it with a laugh. She took his hand in hers and smelt the bouquet.

"Lilies, a blossom for love and death," she said beguilingly.

Back at the pool, two young men had hold of Billy and were wrestling him towards the water.

Veronica tenderly kissed Sean's lips and held on to him. The firmness of her tongue flicked in his mouth. His hand wandered onto her breast and lingered. Momentarily his eye was distracted by Billy, who was midway through the air, arms and legs askew as he splashed down into the pool.

Veronica pulled back and smiled, by the hand she led him into secluded spiny, thick with overgrowth. Once obscured, he kissed her neck and the side of her face. She led him deeper into the woodland, again they kissed, this time more passionately than before. They could hear shrieks and shouts from the pool, as he pulled at her dress. Reaching down, she massaged his groin with one hand and pulled his head to her breast with the other. Sean turned her, lifting her dress, exposing her black lace underwear. Her narrow waist curving into the perfect peach of her hips. He unzipped his fly, pulled out his dick, pushed it between her legs. She placed her hands against an oak tree to steady herself and reaching through she guided him inside her. He rutted like an animal, grabbing her tits hard, from his groin a spark rushed through his nervous system exploding in his brain. He continued humping but Veronica sensed he was spent; it was all over.

"Have you come?" she asked.

Sean, never a considerate lover, said, "Fucking right I have." He paused for a second before laughing out an apologetic. "Yeah, sorry."

THE PICTURE GAME

She laughed, "I'll expect a bit more from you next time."

"I'll tie a knot in it next time." He smiled bashfully, trying to push his still stiff manhood back in his trousers.

He was young and at the mercy of nature and because of her beauty, it gave her power.

Reaching into his jacket he pulled out a serviette and handed to Veronica.

"A gentleman, thank you." She wiped herself, and handed the soiled tissue back.

"Fuck off, I don't want it."

"But it's all yours," Veronica replied slipping it quickly into his pocket.

Sean whipped it back out and flung it to the ground, kicking it under a bush.

Five minutes later Cormac looked up from his conversation with Francis to see Sean and Veronica strolling towards him.

"Where have you been? Sully's been all over looking for you's two."

Francis smiled, backing up his new friend.

"Where is he now?" Veronica asked, casually looking around. "Probably with that bitch."

"No, he was with Billy a few minutes ago," answered Cormac.

"Billy's down by the pool," Veronica responded.

"Well he was with Sully a little while ago, maybe it was half an hour ago," said Cormac, he looked to Francis for confirmation.

Just as Cormac had finished talking, the young man in the Fox mask appeared and hooked arms with Francis.

"Hello darling."

His effeminate voice took the boys by surprise.

"Long time no see." He dropped the mask peering at the group, and particularly Sean and Veronica. "Was it you two I spotted bedding down amongst the bedding plants?" He raised an eyebrow as he continued, specifically to

71

THE PICTURE GAME

Veronica. "Lucky girl."

He was extremely pretty, fair-haired with fine features.

Sean and Veronica did not acknowledge the comment, but both knew exactly how the other felt.

"Oh! I am sorry, please excuse me," his hand touched his face. A silent whisper dripped from his lips, "Oh, my goodness I've done it again." He smirked apologetically and reached over touching Veronica's hand. "Don't worry, I'll keep it zipped," pulling an imaginary zipper across his mouth. "And as for you..."

"This is the Hugo, he's got a big mouth, that he struggles to keep shut," Francis said firmly.

"Never a truer word." Hugo shrieked his face a picture of glee. He languidly stretched out a hand to Cormac, next to Sean and Veronica. "And who are these two gorgeous creatures?"

Hugo looked at Francis for an introduction, who in turn looked to an awestruck Cormac.

"Erm, this is Sean, he's my brother, and this is Veronica, she's erm…" Pausing, "She's a friend."

"Now Francis, as usual, is correct, I am a big mouth, honestly more trouble than it's worth. My name is Victor, but I prefer to be known as Hugo whose work I adore." Seeing the confusion. "Victor Hugo, Les Misérables?" Still no response, "Hunchback of Notre Dame?"

"Oh, I know him, they made a film about him, Desdemona," said Sean.

Hugo leant back and looked at Sean side on, "No, no you're pulling my leg. Isn't he Francis?"

Francis shook his head smiling.

Hugo glanced at Sean and then Francis. Trying to clear up the issue, he went on. "Desdemona was the wife of Othello."

Sean nodded but didn't have a clue what Hugo was on about.

"Now," Hugo waited until he had his audience, "Victor Hugo wrote The Hunchback of Notre Dame, the hunchback saves Esmeralda, don't you remember?" He spoke like a primary school teacher, "Sanctuary, sanctuary!"

"Yes, yes, Victor Hugo, he wrote the book, I remember now, we did it at school, Victor Hugo, The Hunchback of Notre Dame," said Cormac.

"Do you pay for blowjobs?" interrupted Veronica.

Hugo without the slightest hint of embarrassment chipped back a sardonic grin. "Well, I do have a weakness."

Veronica tried to subdue her convulsions, her hic-upy laugh spreading out.

Francis covered his eyes with his hands.

"Oh, my god, she's wonderful. Darling you're wonderful, I want to take you home with me," said Hugo touching Veronica's arm. "I want you to meet my family, I want you all to come to see me, but most of all you. I'll introduce you as my new girlfriend, I think you would make a wonderful beard. What do you think Francis? Blackbeard!" he shrieked with laughter.

They all shared his joke, Veronica once again getting them all going with her peculiar laugh.

"He means a decoy," Francis said explaining. "But Hugo dear, I don't believe there is a woman alive who could pass you off as straight."

"But what fun to try," Hugo giggled.

Hugo continued to entertain with his bawdy camp humour. Eventually, Billy turned up, asking if he could speak to Cormac on his own. The pair wandered off into the gardens.

Billy explained that Sully was on the warpath, confirming Hugo's observation that Sean and Veronica were not as discreet as they may have imagined. Cormac's heart jumped on hearing the news.

"Listen, I'll make out that they were just kissing, he might be alright with that. I know that he's still got the hots for Rose, his ex and if I can get the two of them together." Billy smiled deviously, "Rose is crazy, but she fucks like a starlet. Try and keep Sean and Veronica out of the way for the next hour until I speak to him."

Cormac was nervous, "Well if Sully wants to kick up a stink!" he said aggressively.

Billy, a little taken aback, smiled, palms out placatory fashion. "No, no, I'll make sure nothing happens, he won't do anything in here. I'll speak to him, if I can't get him to cool down, I'll get him out of here. You can borrow my car if needs be, to get home."

Thinking back to the party and the way Sully battered that lad, Cormac wondered if he should have tapered his bravado. Suddenly, he felt sober, nerves jangling the more he thought about the situation. Perhaps this was some sort of plan that Billy and Sully had schemed up. Why did Veronica get in the back of the car with Sean, why had Sully disappeared, and how come Veronica shags Sean in full fucking view of the party?

Turning back towards the house, Billy threw his arm over Cormac's shoulder. "Don't worry about it. Honestly, I'll sort it."

As they walked together, conspiracies, plots and schemes raced through Cormac's mind, his eyes alert as a mongoose on speed.

"Listen, I'm gonna nip upstairs, I'll get Rose. You take Sean and Veronica downstairs to the games room, and I'll see you in a while," said Billy.

There was no sign of the of Sean or Veronica as Cormac scouted around. "Fucking hell, why the fuck did he have to shag her?"

A jolt spun him on his heels.

Big Peter had grabbed his arm, "You've slipped the queer fella."

"Yeah," answered Cormac, "You haven't seen my brother, have you?"

Big Peter's head rocked back. "What's he look like?"

Cormac did his best to describe his Sean, adding, "He

THE PICTURE GAME

was with a tall black girl."

"A tall black, yer say?" Peter's eyes squinted. "No, I don't think so." He turned to the group behind, "Have any of yous seen a tall black girl here?"

They all shook their heads, some glancing around as they did so.

"Was the brother with you earlier on?" Big Peter asked.

"Yeah, him, the black girl, and another lad Sully, with long black hair," said Cormac.

"Black hair yer say, now I know, yes! The black-haired fella was here a while ago. He was talking to somebody." Big Peter looked around the room. "Who was he talking to now?" he asked himself, suddenly inside his mind a light went on, "Yes, that's it, he was talking to you, yourself!" he pointed at Cormac accusingly.

"Don't worry," said Cormac, shaking his head as he moved away. "Fucking idiot," he mumbled to himself.

"I'll tell him you're looking for him." Big Peter called after him.

Cormac scoured the ground floor, but to no avail. He wondered if he should check upstairs, going halfway up, before changing his mind and heading back down.

"Hello? are you lost?" asked a small stocky lady, her voice firm and sharp. She was holding a set of lorgnettes and closely inspected Cormac through them. She was standing beside a man, who looked like a retired brigadier.

"No, I'm looking for somebody. Replied Cormac. "Have you seen a blond lad, a bit smaller than me, he's probably with a black woman."

"Yes, I can help you. They passed by her about an hour ago, they were heading into the ballroom. Isn't that right Clement?"

The Brigadier pursed his lips, "Yes, an hour ago." His arm pointed bayonet like into the ballroom.

Cormac knew he had seen them since, but felt obliged to re-enter. He avoided Big Peter, who he could see out of the corner of his eye and headed straight back out and down towards the games room. "If they're not here," he thought, "I'll take a look around the garden." He opened the door and quickly looked around.

In the corner Hugo, Frances and a grey-haired man were sitting huddled together on a long Chesterfield style couch. The grey-haired man was pushing Hugo's head down into Frances's crotch. Hugo looked up and smiled, before returning to his task.

Francis pushed Hugo off. "You okay?" he called over.

"I was looking for Sean, have you seen him?" Cormac asked, shocked.

Francis let out a long slow breath before answering. "I dunno, he was with that girl, they went back outside." He zipped up the front of his trousers, "Hold on, I'll help you find them."

Before leaving, Cormac glanced back, the older guy was now bent over Hugo's crotch.

"Cormac? Cormac!" Sean called, coming down the stairs.

Cormac looked up. "Where've you been? I've been looking all over for you. Have you spoken to Billy?"

"Yeah, he's upstairs. Reckons Sully's looking for me."

"What's going on?" asked Francis.

"Nothing much, it's just this twat here has fucked up big." Cormac said, eyes boring into his brother's.

"I ain't fucked up," Sean responded aggressively.

"You ain't fucked up." Cormac spat. "You ain't fucked up."

They were now nose to nose.

"You fuck a guy's missus and expect him to slap you on the back and buy you a pint, do you? Do you? Fucking idiot."

Cormac pushed Sean's face backwards. Sean jumped at his brother, fists flying. Cormac got hold of him, easily slinging him to the floor. In a split second, he was on top of him, pinning his arms down. Sean struggled, but Cormac's weight and strength meant he couldn't do much.

Ladies scattered as a few cheering men drew closer. Sean wriggled and twisted and tried to buck but Cormac remained steadfast.

Francis approached, squatting beside them. "Hey, you two, come on, both of you need to get up. Come on!"

"Get this cunt off me," Sean, embarrassed and beaten.

Cormac knew that people were watching, but didn't care. He stared transfixed, intoxicated by the violence, all Cormac could feel was the sensation of his back rising and falling as he inhaled and exhaled. Both control and calm swept through him. There was a hand on his shoulder, shaking him. He leant in to his brother. Suddenly he was wrenched upwards, the force lifted him like a child being scooped up by his father.

"Don't worry folks, it's just a wee bit of a spat." The broad Irish brogue was unmistakably that of Big Peter's. "Ah, like me-self. Can't enjoy a party unless the fists get an outing."

Cormac stumbled as Big Peter tried to land him on his feet. The crowd were smiling, with one or two clapping as Peter restored order.

Billy heard the commotion and rushed over.

"Wasn't you the fool, inviting more than one Irishman from the same family to a party? They'll pick a fight with themselves if they can't find a 'wordy' opponent," said Peter. He laughed, holding both boys by the collar. "Do you want them out of the house altogether?"

"No, they're okay." Billy smiled. "Don't worry folks," he raised his voice for the bystanders. "I'll take care of the savages."

Sean and Cormac did not look at each other. Like naughty children led by the headmaster, both meekly followed Billy up the flight of stairs.

"Fucking hell! To think I was worried about Sully," Billy said, "Fucking Paddies. I could have that bunch of twats down there to a party every night of the week, every week of the year, and all I'd get is maybe a solicitor's

THE PICTURE GAME

letter. Last time Sully punched out a fucking lawyer! And tonight, I'm juggling with all three of you." He grabbed them by the neck, pushing their heads together. "What am I going to do with them, Francis?" he called over his shoulder.

"Fuck knows," Francis laughed.

The heat of the day had now risen to the top of the house, which was like a sauna. Veronica looked up as they entered but remained on a stool. Partly slumped over her was a thin blonde girl, who seemed asleep, her head in Veronica's lap.

"What you been up to?" Billy called over.

Veronica's eyes were hooded and her movements slow. In the centre of the room, a couple of guys were lying flat out on their backs, both bare-chested.

"They're off their faces," said Billy. He crossed the room, "What you been up to?" he repeated.

Veronica looked at the joint in her fingers, taking a while to focus and rolled onto the floor. By her side was a small plastic bag of white powder. Billy picked it up and put it in his pocket.

"Give us a hand," Billy asked to no one in particular. He took hold of Veronica's arms dragging her towards the edge of the bed. As Sean lifted her feet, her gown slipped down revealing long, slender legs, he wanted to ravish her.

"We won't get much out of her for a while. Probably just as well, she's a mouthy bitch," said Billy.

They propped both girls against the bed.

"What have they taken?" asked Sean. "She was fine a few minutes ago."

Billy reached into his pocket, pulling out the white bag. "Not sure," he handing it over. "Open it, but don't sniff, it's not speed."

"Fucking hell, it doesn't look much does it?" Sean shrugged, he passed it over to Cormac.

Billy shook his head slowly from side to side. He looked down at the comatose group. "Bunch of cunts. I'll

THE PICTURE GAME

get them up in a bit, they've still got work."

Cormac went to hand back the white bag.

Billy dipped his finger and tasted it, "White smack, keep it she won't miss it."

He took hold of the thin blonde, Sean once again the arms, dropping her on the bed next to Veronica.

He looked down at the two boys on the floor, "You guys ok?" kicking them on the ankles, they both grunted.

Billy took the smack from Cormac, "Try it, but take it easy." He then lifted a minuscule amount out on the end of his nail. "Put it into a roll-up just like a bit of weed, no more than that, it'll blow your socks off."

Sean took the bag from Cormac and slipped it in his pocket.

79

10
The Drive Home with Francis

The drive home was uneventful. Sean, in the back, slept most of the way. Cormac sat up front with Francis. He was struggling to come to terms with what he had witnessed in the games room. They chatted idly but the conversation struggled. Eventually, Cormac too closed his eyes pretending to be asleep. Dominating his mind was Hugo and how brazenly he went about his pleasures, also spinning were thoughts of Sean, Veronica and Sully. As they neared Coventry, Francis gave Cormac a prod on the thigh.

"You'll have to give me direction."

Cormac made a display of yawning and stretching, despite not sleeping a wink of the journey. "Sorry, mate." He blew out his cheeks, rubbing his face and with exaggerated movements as he directed through the city. The sun had risen but the streets were empty. Cormac pointed out a couple of the local sites, including a few hookers on their way home.

Francis smiled, and glanced over, "A girl's gotta make a living."

Cormac felt stupid, not knowing how to reply. "Just turn right here, this is our road."

Francis pulled up to the kerb.

"Listen, thanks a lot," said Cormac. He pulled out a small roll of cash, peeling off a couple of twenties. "That's a bit of fuel money." He then peeled off another couple,

THE PICTURE GAME

"And that's for you, I appreciate it."

Francis smiled, handing back the cash. "You don't have to pay me."

Cormac took the notes and stuffed them into Francis top pocket.

"You don't have to," said Francis.

There was a noise at the door as it swung open.

Ma appeared, holding the front of her nightdress closed.

"I didn't expect you's till the afternoon, you's are back early," she looked surprised.

"The party's still going, we cleared off," said Sean, slipping past his mother.

She looked over her shoulder as he disappeared into the house. "Was it good?" she called after him.

He did not reply.

Shaking her head in irritation, she looked over to Francis, "Are you coming in for a cup of tea, I'm sorry I don't know your name?"

"It's Francis," he glanced at Cormac.

"Yeah, come in for a cuppa," said Cormac.

Sean had gone straight to bed, leaving Ma entertaining as Cormac made the tea.

"Do you have sugar?" Cormac called through.

"Just one please," came the polite response.

As they chatted Ma asked Francis about the party, how many people were there, what the food was like, who was the fella that invited them.

Francis did his best to answer.

"Was there a lot of pretty girls there?" Ma paused, smiling as she waited for a response. "Wouldn't it be great if the boys managed to get hitched to heiress'. That would get the tongues wagging," she thought and smiled.

"Yes, there was plenty."

"Rich ones?" she clapped her hands in delight and sat forward on her seat, "Expect the boys chatted to a few.

"Oh yes, they were plenty of rich ladies there" replied

81

THE PICTURE GAME

Francis with a wink. "They had them queuing up."

"Ah, just like they're father, nothings so appealing as a queue," her face a picture of pride. She reached over to a photograph on the mantle, smiling with sweet nostalgia, "That's why I fell for Timmy," she passed over the photograph.

It was of Ma and Timmy on a bridge, embracing, each with one eye on the camera, clearly in love.

"It was our honeymoon, I miss him still."

Francis recognising the sadness in her eyes, lowered his head, unsure of what to say.

Sensing Francis' unease, Ma's tone changed, becoming brighter once more.

Cormac arrived with three steaming cups, placing them all on the ring marked coffee table in front of the couch.

Ma who was in her armchair turned on an angle to face Cormac. "Francis was telling me yous had a great time."

Cormac nodded and took a seat.

"Their father was a devil for the ladies," she said.

Cormac rolled his eyes.

"Well they weren't short of admirers," Francis slowly nodded.

Ma liked this polite young man who had taken it upon himself to drop her sons home. He had a calmness and empathy, hopefully he'll be a good friend for Cormac. She was annoyed that Sully was in no fit state to drive home, but was never a big fan of his anyway. "A flash Harry if ever there was one."

"Now, Francis can sleep on the couch. There's no point in him racing off without any sleep." She smiled as if to say, all had been decided. "He can use the telephone to let Billy know." She took a sip of tea and turned to Cormac with a disapproving look. "Letting him go without a wink of sleep."

Ma rose from her seat, "The phone's in the hall," she pointed. "I'm off to bed. I'll throw some blankets down." She rummaged through her bag, handing the key to the

THE PICTURE GAME

phone lock to Cormac.

Amusingly her dressing gown was caught between the cheeks of her arse as she disappeared upstairs.

Cormac looked over at Francis, they both smiled.

"I better check if it's ok with Billy," said Francis, rising, he went into the hall and closed the door.

A soft thud came from the bottom of the stairs. Cormac lifted the blankets, placing them on the couch. Quietly he went to the hall door to eavesdrop.

Francis, "Okay mate, I'll see you sometime tomorrow. I mean today."

The phone clicked.

Cormac quickly moved away, and began arranging the blankets.

"It's fine, Billy says he doesn't need the car for a couple of days." He waved Cormac forward, lowering his voice to a whisper. "He asked me to tell you that he's put the three of them all in the same bed: Veronica, Sully and Rose."

Cormac smiled.

With Francis so close, he felt a longing to touch him.

Francis unbuttoned his collar, sat on the arm of the sofa and pulled off his shirt, he was lean and fit. He paused as he unbuttoned the waistband of his trousers. "What time do you normally get up?"

"Don't worry, whenever," said Cormac, trying to act nonchalant. "I'm fucked."

Francis folded his clothes into a tidy square and turned to Cormac.

Cormac felt confused, he knew what he wanted to do, he wanted to touch him, to kiss him, to fuck him, but his soul was cursing his heart, never dare, never do. "A fucking queer, a fucking queer, a perverted cunt," he thought. "Why can't I be straight?"

Francis, raised his hand and touched the back of his Cormac's head, a barely perceivable resistance warned him off. Cormac had peeked through the door of

83

discovery, but fearful, could not enter. They stood facing one another for what could have been a lifetime, and yet it was no more than a click of two fingers. Finally, Francis kissed his forehead and whispered.

"See you in the morning."

11
The After Eight

The team was Sean, John, with two new sellers, Tom and Pam. Tom was pale with a mop of frizzy strawberry blond hair, Pam, slim with a sleek bob. Stan once again was driving. They were heading south towards London and decided to have an early dinner at the motorway services. On entering, John and Sean spotted a couple of familiar faces and wandered over.

Leroy and Murphy were working the fruit machines, it was a scam. Murphy had memorised the barrels of the machine, knowing what fruits were hidden, so once it flashed up a nudge, nine times out of ten they would bring home a win. But that was only half the trick. Leroy was renowned for his use of a garden strimmer wire to clock up free games. With the dexterity of a safecracker, he would slip the wire in the coin slot, tripping a sensor, fooling the machine that coins had been fed through. This allowed them to play for free until the machine was cleaned out.

There was still money to be had at it, but life was getting harder. Manufacturers were wising up, putting alarms into the slot. Electronic machines were just beginning to come through, but there were enough old mechanical ones out there to make strimming another cottage industry for a ne'er-do-well.

Sean and John stood watching, Leroy and Murphy were always happy to see a few friendly faces, extra cover from prying eyes. They could clean out a machine in minutes,

THE PICTURE GAME

and with pockets laden move onto the next. They operated mostly up and down the motorway services, occasionally pubs, but with wary landlords, it was more difficult.

Murphy asked where they were selling, suggesting they could meet up later. They agreed the Black Cat café, just after Northampton. Sean and John knew that Murphy and Leroy wouldn't be there, Murphy and Leroy knew that there wasn't a cat in hells chance of Sean and John turning up, nonetheless, the plan was made.

Calling, "Laters man," they parted company.

In the cafe, they ordered the same meal of pie, chips and beans. Looking around they spotted Stan, who waved them over.

Tom asked how much Murphy and Leroy were on.

"Pockets full man, good money," replied John laughing, adding, "We're in the wrong game."

Sean, "Nah, I bet they don't clear more than fifty or sixty between them."

Tom was trying to distract Pam from her magazine, but his efforts were falling on deaf ears, she was engrossed.

"No, I think they do," said John, "Our kid did it for a while before he went to Spain, it's good money."

Sean shook his head as he stuffed his face with a mouthful of chips.

"How's he doing out there, he's married a German, ain't he?" Sean asked.

"Yeah, Marla, she's beautiful." John smiled, "Fucked if I know what's she doing with our Kenny. Apart from that twelve-inch dick, he ain't got a lot going for him."

The boys laughed, looking to Pam for a reaction, she was oblivious, absorbed in her magazine. They finished their food and left. They were already close to Hitchin, so they were in no hurry. Hitchin was where the prints were made. Most sellers were scared to work there, thinking that everyone in the town knew the score. But the rewards were high despite the risk, as it wasn't knocked so regularly. And if worst came to worst and you did get pulled by the

THE PICTURE GAME

rozzers, it was only a night in a cell, with a burger for breakfast.

It was mid-September and the evenings were still bright. Stan was laying out the sets, Sean, John and Tom sat down on the kerbside sharing a joint, while Pam stayed in the car.

With a grin Sean stood up and wandered over to Stan. He unzipped his flies and pulled out his cock, hovering it close to Stan's left ear. At the sound of laughter, Stan turned his head, catching the cock on his cheek.

The lads roared with laughter.

"Fuck off you cunts," he said as he swiped at Sean, adding "fucking bunch of perverts."

Sean jumped back, "While you're down there Stan, while you're down there," pushing his hips in Stan's direction. "Go on give it a nosh!"

Stan raised his hand covering the exposed side of his face but couldn't help laughing, "Fuck me, like a cock, but only smaller."

"Fuck off that's a beast!" Sean said, pursuing Stan.

Stan struck out his hand, catching Sean's foreskin with the end of his fingers.

"Ah, fucking hell, Stan!" Sean's voice pitched with pain. "You've cut the fucker. Look, he's fucking cut me."

Tom and John were in stitches, full tilt back on the kerb as Sean approached cock in hand.

Pam looked up from her magazine, "Serves you right," she shouted from the back of the car.

Sean frowned, wiping spittle over his injured member, gently easing it back into his jeans.

Stan chuckled satisfyingly to himself.

Ten minutes later they were on the doors. Sean was on the opposite side of the road to Pam, who had wandered off as he adjusted himself. He watched as she knocked her first door. She delivered her lines, the punters swallowed it and invited her in.

Before entering, she looked back, with a look that said,

THE PICTURE GAME

"What are you fucking looking at?"

Sean flashed back an exaggerated smile as the door closed.

"Upwards and onwards," he sighed, hitching his set on to his hip. "Hello, sorry to disturb you…"

The night was uneventful, apart from getting swung at by an old man with a walking stick. The old man complained that it was too late to be calling on people's doors and he didn't like Sean's backchat either.

"I would have knocked the old cunt out if I could have got past his stick, he was like a fucking ninja," Sean laughed later with his friends.

Overall, it was a bummer, Sean only shifted two meds and four smalls. At nine o'clock he sat down on the kerbside and was happy when Stan pulled up. They got back to Coventry for ten-thirty. Wednesday night was the 'After Eight,' a club in the heart of the City. The beer was watered down, but at a pound a pint the place was busy. John knew most of the bouncers in town from his boxing days and was well-liked. He led them straight to the front. Barry, a small Irish guy with crazy brown eyes, was on. They embraced and shared a few pleasantries. Despite the queue, the club was far from being full. That's the way a lot of clubs worked it back then, queues, queues, queues. It was disco night, the D.J. was clearly a big fan of K.C. and the Sunshine Band and was running through their back catalogue. Sully was sitting at a table just below a strobe light which crept over his body, creating a strange halo effect. On spotting them, he came over. Sean felt nervous as he approached. He hadn't seen him since the London party.

"How's it going?" Sully asked. He was carrying a near-empty pint glass and swigged the rest down as he leant on the bar.

"Do you want one?" Sean asked, pointing at the empty pint glass.

He was watching Sully's face, trying to read his mood.

88

THE PICTURE GAME

But Sully wasn't the type to give much away. Sean noticed that the shoulder of Sully's jacket was split, the sleeve flopping over at the top.

"Cool man, lager," Sully replied, leaning in towards Sean. "Where have yous been?"

Sean said, "Hitchin again, not bad. Did you do a shift?" Wondering what had happened to Sully's jacket.

"Cardiff, Sully shouted over the music, "It was a bummer, pissed down for most of the night. We jacked in after an hour."

The barman had already served up the order and was standing expressionless, waiting to be paid.

"Sorry mate!" Sean excused himself, reaching into his pocket, he pulled out a tenner.

The barman disappeared to the till.

"You and me's gotta talk," said Sully. As he spoke, he moved his arm to the back of Sean's neck, giving him a firm squeeze.

Sean felt nervous as he picked up his change.

The opening bars of, "*That's the way, uh-huh, uh-huh! I like it, that's the way...*" by KC blasted across the room. A fat lass in a blue satin dress grabbed her handbag, heading to the dance floor. Her friends close behind. Sully grabbed the arse of a petite brunette, the last to pass.

She glared at him, "Fuck off."

Sully blew a kiss as she followed her friends. "Fucking arse on that bitch. You'd sink your teeth in, wouldn't you mate?" he said laughing.

Sean eyed the girl, there was no arguing, her arse was a peach.

A young punk couple, both jet black hair, both wearing makeup, eyed Sean and Sully with a look of disgust.

"What you fucking looking at?" said Sully, glaring at the couple.

Sean joined in with the bad-boy stare.

The punk stood his ground until his girlfriend pulled him away.

THE PICTURE GAME

"Who is he?" asked Sean

"Fuck knows, some cunt," replied Sully, loud enough so all could hear.

Sean laughed, "Arsehole, dressed like that." Then tugging on Sully's frayed shoulder. "What's happened to you?"

"I know, you can't get a decent coat these days, I only bought it at Christmas, pile of crap!" said Sully, tucking in the threads. "Shite, absolute fucking shite, I paid fifty quid for it."

A flash of light flew past Sean and something glanced off his forehead. The crowd opened up, people scattered. Sully was being backed up by the young punk, who had a broken glass in his hand, repeatedly punching it into Sully's face. Calling for security, the DJ stopped the music. Sean froze, as he watched as John walloped the punk on the side of the head. The punch did not have any effect as the onslaught continued on Sully. Then, as in delayed response, the punk turned to face John, who hit him again, dropping the guy to his knees. Barry the bouncer arrived along with another guy, built like a brick shithouse. They grabbed both the fallen punk and Sully, bum-rushing them through the crowd.

Sully was in a bad way; his head had been gashed open all around his left eye with blood freely spurting from a wound within his hairline. Barry was guarding the punk behind the ticket booth. John managed to grab hold of him by the hair, briefly dragging him out, a flurry of boots and fist were landing. Barry quickly bundled the punk back, placing himself between him and John.

A barmaid arrived with a beer towel and delicately dabbed at Sully's wounded head.

Barry shouted over, "Hold it tight on,"

The barmaid grimaced but did as she was told.

John swapped places with her. "You alright mate?" he asked.

Sully looked dazed, saying he was fine and attempted

90

THE PICTURE GAME

to walk back into the club.

The girl punk was crying. "Leave him alone," she shouted.

Other bouncers had cordoned the area off pushing onlookers back.

"You'll need to get him to the hospital," the barmaid said to John.

John briefly lifted the towel to inspect the wound, before pressing it firmly back onto Sully's skull. "We're gonna have to get you down to the hospital mate."

"Fuck off, I'm fine," Sully replied, half-heartedly. "Where's the guy who hit me?"

John looked over. The punk was sitting on the floor of the ticket booth, apparently unconcerned. Spots and smears of blood decorated his Ramones T-shirt. He caught John's eye and grinned as he examined his fists for cuts.

"Lisa, Lisa," he shouted.

Once more he attempted to launch himself over the top of the ticket booth, only to be wrestled to the floor by Barry.

"You're a smart-arse cunt, aren't ya?" Barry said, in a strong Northern Irish accent. "Just fucking stay in there."

Sean took a crafty swipe.

The punk tried to lunge at Sean but was hauled about like a ragdoll by the bouncer.

"Let him go," said Sully. "Just let the fucker go, I don't want any more shit just, let him go!" he screamed.

Barry glanced over; eyes as black as coal. He then calmly nodded and waved over to the huge bouncer to push the crowd out of the reception area.

The bouncer followed Barry's instructions.

Barry faced the young punk, he raised his left hand, the punk turned, only to be hit with two vicious straight rights knocking him clean out. Barry dragged the stricken boy out from the booth, blood oozing from his nose and mouth. Once outside, he propped him against the wall. Barry squatted down, slapping the punk's face back to semi-consciousness.

"Don't fucking come in here again… yer fucking hear me?" Pulling at the boy, he jerked him forward, the boy's head jolted back. Barry repeated his warning.

The punk nodded a surly "Alright."

There was a time when Barry loved nothing better than a good ol' tear-up. Violence, whether dishing it out or receiving it was in his blood. But the years had mellowed him. He was sick of the job, seedy clubs and this disco shite. He pulled the boy to his feet, who was showing signs of recovery.

Barry stood motionless, as Lisa helped her man away. Cold and neutral, his eyes followed as they rounded the corner. He turned towards the door, calling out to a group he recognised. "No chance lads."

12
To the Hospital

Despite his wounds Sully was in good spirits, Sean had volunteered to go with him. As they walked occasionally Sully would stop to wipe the blood that dripped into his eyes from the makeshift bandage.

Under the flyover which contoured the city centre, they found a bench.

"How deep is it?" said Sully, pulling up the bandage.

"Don't fucking do that, you'll fucking… you'll bleed to death," said Sean as he looked at the semi congealed blood stuck in Sully's hair. "I think I can see your skull."

Sully let out a hearty laugh, causing the blood to drip faster. He rubbed some of the sticky blood through his fingers and tasted it.

Sean was repulsed. "Best if you leave it. Come on, let's get to the hospital."

Sean rose to his feet, drew in the damp air and watched his breath tumble before him. He didn't want to be here, he wanted to be at home, warm and safe. "Come on!" he called, taking a few steps, before glancing back, hoping Sully had followed.

Sully was gazing into space, his forefinger and thumb playing with the sticky mess. "Did you fuck Veronica?" he called out.

Sean heard but decided that he hadn't. He stuck both hands in his pockets and shouted. "Come on you cunt, let's go."

Sully sat motionless, he glanced over at Sean then back

THE PICTURE GAME

out into the distance. He liked Sean, who was quick to laugh; he had a fragility and openness. This was opposed to Cormac; whose manner was far too cool for Sully. He knew that Sean had shagged Veronica, she had told him. "Bitch," he thought. "She'll get hers soon enough." Adrenaline had subsided, his head was now hurting, he knew a dull ache would follow. Pressing his fingers onto the open wound he immersed himself into the pain. Like a drug it cleared his mind. He tasted the cool air as it travelled up his nostrils hitting the back of his throat and down into his lungs. In this meditative state, he felt calm. He sat for a few more seconds. His breath passed over his lips, warming his nose. Reaching up he caught hold of a piece of loose flesh and gently tugged. There was a twinge, he pulled harder, a smart pain, but the flesh held firm.

"What the fuck are you doing?" Sean called over.

"You need to get to the hospital mate, your heads pissing."

The blood had followed the contours of his face, coating his shirt and was dripping onto his jeans. He leant forward allowing it to pool, it quickly filled the ground between his shoes, how black it looked.

A police car cruised by; a blockhead of a copper called across. Sully recognised him. It was Paddy Kincaid, a wanker, who wouldn't think twice to stick the boot in to make his point. Fuck all if it weren't for his uniform.

Sully responded as if greeting an old friend. "How you doing, Paddy?" he laughed over.

"Are you Ok?" asked the Kincaid.

"Yeah, pissed, tripped on a kerb," replied Sully. "We're just heading down to the hospital."

The copper joked back, "Well if it's only your head, no harm done. You're ok though?" He knew differently, but didn't want to have to wipe Sully's blood off the back seats.

Both Sully and Sean laughed.

THE PICTURE GAME

"Yeah, fine," said Sully, rising to his feet.

"Do you need a lift?" said Kincaid, knowing there was no chance of Sully getting in the car.

"No, I'm fine, Sean's looking after me," he nodded in Sean's direction, who raised his hand.

"Fair enough," Kincaid called back, "get yourself to the hospital."

The cop car slowly moved off.

They watched as it looped around the roundabout, heading back into town, siren and light flashing on as it set sail over the traffic lights.

Sully called out "Wanker," well out of earshot.

"Come on!" he called, heading off like a steam-train.

Sean picked up his pace drawing alongside.

Sully pulled a raffle ticket from the dispenser and sat down next to an old man in pyjamas. The old man looked vacant and confused, a few days growth of grey bristle, dried blood in the wrinkles and creases of his mouth. He was being looked after by a younger red-haired man, who could have been the old man's son.

"Fucking place this" Sully said sitting back on his seat, as he gazed around at the walking wounded.

"You want a Mars Bar?" Sean called out, from a brightly coloured vending machine.

Sully thought for a while, "Do they have a Turkish Delight?"

13
Francis's Ghost

Ma was moving around downstairs, singing "Tura Ra loo Ra Loo Rai," a soft Irish lullaby. Birds were singing their morning chorus as the tyres hissed on the wet road outside.

Cormac stared blankly at the bedroom ceiling, eyes soft and unfocused. Something caught his eye, he lowered his gaze.

"What the fuck!"

On the end of his bed with his knees pulled up to his chest was Francis, his face and body white and ghostly. Cormac jolted, his heart leapt and his eyes cracked open. Francis was no longer there, the room was empty, no birds, no soft lullaby. Terrified he blinked his way back into reality.

"No, he wasn't there, he couldn't have been here," he thought.

A panic seized him, cautiously, he peered under his bed, half expecting to see Francis' alabaster body, there was an old dusty suitcase and the remains of a broken Scalextric. He looked across beneath his brother's bed, only the remnants of an old carpet. He let out a sigh and took in a slow deep breath. There was no sign of Francis and had not been for weeks. With his heart still racing, he felt for a heartbeat, and was surprised as it drummed out a steady rhythm. It was a Sunday, so he lay for a minute or two calming himself, before going downstairs.

Sean was already at the breakfast table, Cormac sat

THE PICTURE GAME

down opposite.

Sean had been waiting for Cormac to tell him about Sully.

"You should have seen it, blood was pissing out, I thought he was gonna die," said Sean, gesturing as he reached across the table for toast. "Shall we'll call over later, he said he'll be home."

Still not quite himself, Cormac responded with a nod. He didn't feel hungry so only played with his slice of toast. "You'd never seen the guy before?"

"No, he was a punk, weird looking," Sean slurped down some tea. "I mean, he looked good but weird. He had eyeliner on." Sean ran the tip of his little finger over his eyelid as he spoke.

Cormac looked over, "What a cunt."

Ma entered from the kitchen, a piece of sausage in her hand, the other half on a side plate. She ate with delicate bites, it was all her false teeth could manage.

"What did you say?" she spoke sternly.

With his arm hanging over the edge of his chair, Sean smiled as his brother squirmed. Cormac's eyes flicked towards his mother.

Ma glared at her him, "If I hear that sort of language in this house, there's the door." Her eyes fixed stubbornly on Cormac.

Sean burst out laughing, enjoying Cormac's humiliation. Then in his brother's defence, "He didn't say anything, we were just talking about our mate."

Ma didn't move, Cormac cowered, glanced over to Sean with exaggerated fear.

"He didn't say anything," Sean repeated, the picture of innocence.

Cormac leant forward, elbows on the table as he nibbled on the toast.

Ma had made her point but to underline it. "If ever I hear that sort of language from either of you," she glared back and forth between the two. "Yous can clear out, do ya

THE PICTURE GAME

hear me!"

She turned and sat on her favourite armchair, finishing her sausage. "And clear away the table before yous go."

14
Plain or Salt & Vinegar

They arrived at Sully's at four o'clock. The day had clouded over, but it was still warm. Veronica opened the door, wearing a short satin dressing gown with a Japanese floral print. If she was embarrassed, she managed to disguise it well.

"Hi guys, come in. Sully, it's your picture mates!" she called out.

"Who?" shouted Sully, adding, "Bring them in," before she answered.

"It's Sean and his brother," she glanced over her shoulder as they walked through. "Sorry mate, my brain's gone foggy. I've forgotten your name."

"Cormac."

"Cormac," she shouted.

Sully was wearing a grey t-shirt and boxer shorts. He was stretched out over a tatty green leather armchair and busy skinning up, a four-pack of lager nestled beside him. The top of his head was bandaged, with a dressing over his left eye. His face was swollen, purple and blacked in parts. On the floor a pile of bloodstained tissue.

"Hey, fuck, I didn't expect to see you two," he grinned. "Sit down." Sully pointed towards an old couch which matched the chair he was sitting on. Spliff in hand, he reached down and pulled loose a couple of cans, passing them to Veronica, who was perched on his chair. She rose and handed them to Sean and Cormac. Sully watched

THE PICTURE GAME

closely as she approached Sean, looking for some sort of acknowledgement, but neither showed any sign of connection.

Cormac broke the tension, laughing, "Fucking hell mate, you look like a cross between Mr Potato Head and the Elephant Man."

"Fuck off," said Sully.

Sully lit his spliff, letting out a throaty cough, inhaling the fumes deeply, he coughed again and spat out a bit of tobacco onto the floor.

"Doesn't hurt though," he tapped around his forehead to prove his point. "They've given me these fuckers," he pulled out a small bottle of tablets from the side of the cushion and shook the bottle, adding with a laugh. "You could put an axe in my head, and I wouldn't feel it." He took another drag from his spliff, and coughed out some smoke rings, watching as they rose towards the ceiling. He passed the spliff to Veronica.

Cormac let out a loud burp as he sat back on the couch. "Do you know who the guy was?" Lifting the can from his chest to his lips, he burped again, "Fucking gassy, this shit," he said looking at the can.

Sully laughed, "That's good beer, Veronica brought it over for me, gently stroking her neck.

"No, he was a crazy fuck though, I only called him a cunt."

Veronica raised her eyebrows.

The boys laughed.

Cormac glanced across at his brother, then back to Sully.

"I thought he was queer," said Sean.

"Only as queer as you two fucks. Nah, he wasn't queer," said Sully shaking his head, he winked at Veronica. "Tom and Huck need to get out more, spend a bit of time in the big city." He grinned, "You get guys like that all the time in London. They ain't queer, that's the look." He watched them, "A pair of simpletons," he

THE PICTURE GAME

thought to himself. "Nah, he wasn't queer..." then added, "Maybe he was, I don't know."

Veronica handed the spliff back and wandered out of the room. Sean kept his eyes down but watched as she left.

"Hey, thanks for hanging around last night," Sully said, raising his can in Sean's direction. "It was a pretty fucked up night really. I hate that place. Something always goes off. He paused before taking another drag and lowered his voice, "Listen, mate, I know you've got a thing for her," nodding in the direction of the kitchen. "I ain't gonna fucking row with you, I wanted to speak to you last night but listen, just watch yourself."

Sean looked like the little boy caught with his hand in the biscuit barrel.

Sully broke out laughing. "Go for it, I don't give a fuck, but just warning you." He sat back in his chair and took a swig of beer watching Sean for a reaction.

Sean glanced towards his brother. Cormac was weighing up the situation. Sully was never short of women, that was true but he wasn't the sort to share, there had to be some reason.

"Fancy a blast?" Sully said offering the spliff.

"No mate I'm okay, stick with the beer," Cormac said taking another swig.

Sean took the spliff, taking a few puffs before handing it back. Veronica returned carrying another pack of beer along with a mixed bag of crisps.

"What flavour?" she asked, ripping open the pack.

"Bacon for me," said Sully holding out his hand.

Veronica dipped into the bag, rummaged through and threw him a bag.

"You can have chicken, no bacon left."

Sully looked confused but didn't say anything.

"What about you two?" she asked.

As she spun around, her gown lifted slightly, revealing her long, lean thighs. Sean tried not to look but couldn't help himself.

101

THE PICTURE GAME

Cormac answered first. "Salt and vinegar please."

"Me too," said Sean.

"Someone's gonna have to have plain. No salt and vinegar left," she teased.

Waving a bag of plain crisps, she deliberated for a second then threw them at Cormac, Then dipping once more into the bag, she pulled out salt and vinegar, launching it at Sean.

"Thanks," they said in unison.

Veronica sat on the arm of Sully's chair, cracked open a can of lager, and began munching on her crisps. Things were quiet for a while as they all chomped away.

Breaking the silence, "What you two up to today?" Veronica asked.

"Nothing much, just got to check some orders, get a few things sorted for the morning," answered Cormac.

Sean looked awkward, "Fuck all really." He sat further back into the couch.

Urged by Sully, Sean went over the previous night's events. Veronica was interested in the details, particularly the fight, constantly asking questions. It was obvious that Sully had only given her the bare minimum, aware that a story about you is always better told by someone else. He looked over approvingly as Sean generously embroidered and wove Sully's heroics in letting the lad go. Next, she wanted to see the scars and unwrap Sully's bandaged head to examine his scalp. His head was shaved in parts, the wounds had not scabbed over, zigzag stitches along with black lines of semi congealed blood oozed. Veronica pulled a face but continued searching through his hair for any missed wounds.

Cormac approached, "Ah! That looks disgusting."

Sean watched intently, as Veronica fussed and fawned over Sully, wishing it was him.

102

15
The Elastic Inn

"It's someone for you," Ma said, opening the door to the living room.

"Who?" said Sean.

Ma shrugged her shoulders.

It was the evening of the same day they had seen Sully.

On reaching the door, he was surprised to see Veronica.

"Hi, how you doing?" her face lit up with a smile.

Veronica spun on her heel, looking away briefly, then back. Sean stood dumbstruck, hands stuffed into his jean pockets, shoulders forward, bashfully grinning.

"Yeah, I'm good," he finally replied, acting on a stage he was unfamiliar with.

"What you doing?" Veronica asked.

"Nothing, just chilling."

She leant in, maybe only six inches from his face, came close to kissing him, then moved away. "Maybe you might wanna go out." Her hands were crossed in front of her hips, her body swaying this way, then that. "Are there any decent pubs around here?"

Sean's thoughts were clearing, the headlights had begun to dim. "Only old man's pubs."

"I don't mind. I like old men," a devilish look in her eye. "Come on, let's go," she said. Her look was challenging, asking questions, did he measure up?

Arm in arm, they walk down to the Elastic Inn. Some say love is madness, whether or not that is true, Sean was

103

THE PICTURE GAME

truly smitten and found himself at the pub, unaware of how he got there.

A few well pickled barflies looked up as they entered.

"Alright mate," said Veronica to one who was probably thirty but looked closer to sixty. They took a seat at the far corner, next to the jukebox. A weasel-faced barman wiped the table and collected the empty glasses. Veronica thanked him placing her glass on the varnished surface. Two seconds later he was back with fresh beermats.

"You're keen," she joked with a hint of flirtation.

"Always keen me," he winked, returning behind the bar.

"That's how I like my men," Veronica laughed.

The 'green eyed monster,' nudged Sean, "Arsehole," Sean thought as he glared across at the grinning barman.

They drank and chatted, all the usual twenty questions new lovers ask, with kisses when no one was watching. Veronica told him about her herself. She'd been bought up in care homes, staying odd months here and there with foster parents. Her dad was a Moroccan sailor, who had fell for her mum when he was on weekend leave in Portsmouth. Veronica didn't meet him until he came over for her First Communion when she was eight.

You Catholic? Sean asked.

"Not really, Veronica replied. "It was the family I was with, my dad's Muslim, whenever he comes over, he's always getting out his prayer mat, they have to pray to Mecca every day."

"Fuck me, that's a lot, I didn't think they were religious."

Looking directly at Sean, "Hey, did you know it was Veronica who wiped Jesus's face before he was crucified?"

"Yeah, I think that's got something to do with the shroud," said Sean.

"Yeah, I think so. No, no, it weren't that, that was something else," she said. "the shroud was once he was

104

THE PICTURE GAME

dead."

"Fuck me, yeah, gotta be," Sean replied.

Veronica said she hoped one day to move to Morocco to be with her dad and meet her step sister. Her mother was a hippy from the sixties and was still living the hippy lifestyle now on a kibbutz in Israel. Veronica's favourite music was soul, Diana Ross her idol. Sean talked about his dad, and of how Ma had brought them up on her own. He had an uncle in New York and was gonna go out there one day.

On the mention of New York, Veronica told him about one of her friends, a Latin guy called Longshot, absolutely beautiful and gay, who disappeared in New York. The word was he got caught up in heavy porn scene.

"Totally disappeared, he was *soo* pretty," Veronica said. "You'd make a good gay porn star," she teased.

"Fuck off, I'm not a shirt lifter" Sean said, but still took it as a compliment.

My pretty boy," she planted a sloppy kiss on his lips. "I'll be your manager; we'll just avoid the snuff movies."

"Fuck off and get killed!" Sean said firmly.

"No, I said we won't do them," she grinned, "Well maybe only the odd one," laughing.

Alcohol had softened Sean's opinion of the barman, so much so, he bought him a drink as the last orders bell went.

Half an hour later, "Drink up folks, off to your beds," was called out. They looked around, realising they were the only ones left.

"We better get a move on," said Sean.

"To your place," said Veronica, as she rose unsteadily on her feet.

"Yeah, I think so… sure," replied Sean, now filled with Dutch courage. He knew that Ma would not like it if she found out, but what the hell.

The barman called, "Enjoy yourselves," and waved a cheerio.

THE PICTURE GAME

They walked, they talked, they stumbled, and tumbled, holding each other up whenever they could.

Sean sang a few Neil Young songs, with Veronica joining in with the odd line. They kissed, they fondled, not making love, but dirty sex in a darkened alley.

"I love you," slipped from his lips. His heart flew free but only for a moment, as no sooner, his mind put it back on the leash.

She raised her face to his, smiled and kissed him gently.

After a few unsuccessful attempts, he pushed the key in the door. Placing a finger to his lips with a "shush," they tip-toed through the sitting room and upstairs. Veronica stripped down to her underwear as they snuggled into bed. They made love again, this time silently, for fear of waking Cormac.

At about six Veronica woke Sean with a kiss, saying she would have to go. She had some modelling work that Sully had lined up in London but would be back in a week or so and they could meet up.

Silently closing the door behind them they made their way to the train station. Veronica said laughing that she'd send him a postcard from London.

A smiling Sean jotted down his address, hoping she wasn't joking.

16
Mad and Contagious

Sean convinced himself that he wasn't expecting a card, sure, she was only joking, but still looked out every day for the postman. A week passed, he just had to sit tight, another few days, still nothing.

Cormac said, "it's just another bird, what's the problem?"

But Veronica wasn't just another bird, she was under his skin and whatever spell she had cast, it was controlling him. Sean asked if Cormac would take him over to Sully's, Cormac agreed to go at the weekend.

They set off early Saturday morning, in the van on the way over, Sean ran through the possible scenarios. What if she was there? What if she wasn't? What if Sully went for him? This he considered a strong possibility and worried him.

Cormac said no big deal, that Sully wouldn't start on the pair of them. Their plan was to say they had just done a delivery and thought they would check on the patient. Cormac would do the talking.

Sully seemed pleasantly surprised as he welcomed them in. His face was still on the yellow side from the faded bruising, but he looked a whole lot better. They followed him through to the front room, sitting on the same tired couch. Tea or beer was offered, both chose beer. Sully went to his kitchen, returning with a four-pack. The conversation was vague, business and football, hopefully, the Sky Blues would get a good start to the season. Cormac asked Sully how his face was, Sully checked his lumps and bumps in the warped wall mirror.

"It's this one up here that's the worst," he ducked, exposing a nasty wound on his hairline. "Yeah, this one opened up. Still fucking sore," running his fingers gingerly across it.

He asked if either of them had since seen the punk guy who had done him in. Neither had, but boastfully made it plain that if they did, they would make sure he would suffer a few lumps and bumps as way of retribution.

Cormac was considering how best to broach the subject of Veronica.

"Not too soon," he remembered his uncle would say when taking them fishing as kids. "Take your time boys, let them settle and forget you are there." After a half an hour of talking shite, Cormac asked, "Hey, how's it going with that bird?"

Sean watched Sully closely for a response.

But Sully was a smart guy and knew this was coming, thinking to himself, "Checking in on the patient, who were they trying to fool." With a confused expression, he replied, "Which one?"

"Fucking hell, true enough mate," Cormac laughed. "I forgot we're in the presence of Don Juan O'Sullivan. You know, the horney half-caste one for fuck's sake."

"Ah, you mean Veronica, the bird that was here?" Sully grinned.

"Yeah, you still with her?" Cormac said.

Sully thought for a moment running through his options. "Hey, listen, I've been upfront with you, haven't I?" he nodded at Sean. "I know she went to see you," tapping his nose, he laughed.

Sean put down his beer, as adrenaline heightening his senses.

Sully raised his palms. "Cool man, cool. Listen, I don't need any trouble. Like I said, she's a great fuck, but she'll

THE PICTURE GAME

pull you down. It's the way some birds are." He paused for a few moments, before continuing, "You're a decent kid Sean, I like you."

Sean was taken aback, "Has she been in touch?" he asked in a whisper.

"I had a phone call last week." Sully replied, reaching across for the tobacco tin on the arm of his chair, skinning up, he went on. "She's staying in Hammersmith; said she was doing some modelling. She asked about you." Sully looked over.

"What did she say? Sean replied.

"Just if I'd seen you," said Sully. "I told her no."

She told me she was doing a modelling job for you," Sean was acting like he didn't care, but it was as plain as the nose on his face that he was upset.

Sully shrugged his shoulders, "I haven't organised any job." He lowered his voice as he went on, "You must have known when you guys first met her, she's fucking schizo?"

Sean shuffled uncomfortably. Veronica hadn't struck him as schizo, but then again, he didn't know anybody who was. He laughed in agreement, trying to match the tone. But his heart was sinking. "It's always the best-looking…..." he said feebly and glanced over at his brother.

"Fucking right," said Cormac, clapping him on the shoulder.

"Too fucking right," Sully added. "She's a fucking A.1 nutter, forget her mate."

Sean took a long slug of beer and laughed. He knew that to maintain his dignity, he had to drop the conversation.

The next half hour involved more shite, football, business and running down women. The boys rose to leave.

Sully called out. "Don't let her get in your head."

In the van, Sean asked Cormac what he thought.

109

THE PICTURE GAME

"Sully was probably right," he said. "If she was interested, she'd have been in touch." But Cormac thought something was strange about Sully's tone, "Maybe too open, why would he say that about her?" He looked across to his brother, offering, "Perhaps he doth protest too much."

On the journey home Sean's mind played its game, working away at him. In his mind's eye, he could see her clearly, prostituting herself to fat ugly men, handing over their filthy cash, leering, touching, carnally embracing. The thought both disgusted and excited him.

Ma was in the kitchen. "You boys like a bit of soup?" she asked, reaching up for bowls.

"I'm okay," Sean said. He poured himself a glass of water, sinking it straight down.

It was unlike Sean to refuse food, "Are you feeling ok son?" she touched his forehead with the back of her hand, and looked into his face. "I don't think you're running a temperature."

"I'm fine. I just don't feel hungry." Sean paused. "I'll have some later."

"You'll have some later?" Looking curiously at her son, "What's the matter with yer?" she snapped.

"I'm fine, I'm fine. I'm just getting some water." He refilled his glass, and walked off into the front room.

"What's the matter with him?" she asked Cormac, who was buttering a slice of bread.

"He's okay. I think he's just a bit tired," replied Cormac.

Ma looked across, "Have you upset him?" Her face full of inquisition.

Cormac denied it had anything to do with him, but Ma had it in her mind something had happened. She glared at her elder son.

"Don't look at me. It's not me!" adding, "ask him." Cormac looked down at the bowl of steaming hot soup, dipped the bread, and wandering off.

THE PICTURE GAME

She shook her head and wondered, Sean had always been a cry-baby, happy or sad he would cry, couldn't control his emotions. It was only as he got older, that he'd managed some sort of balance. Cormac was different, he had an inner strength and independence. But Sean was fragile, a fragility she worried about.

Sean mulled things over for the rest of the week. The love sick spell had infected his thoughts, each day releasing more of its venom. He spilled out his confusion to John.

John listened, not saying much but when Sean had finished, said he knew that Sully had a few girls loaned out down there, so maybe yeah? There was no maybe with Sean, he was convinced she was being kept in a brothel, and Sully had something to do with it. He asked if John would help to find her and get her out.

John said yeah, as long as that's what she wanted, because if Veronica didn't want to leave, they'd have to kidnap her, which was a totally different kettle of fish. Sean asked if John could get Leroy to come along, a little more muscle. John said Leroy was too close to Sully, so nah. John said he'd go see Sully at the weekend and find out what was going on.

Sully shat himself, when John called over and said that whatever Veronica was doing, was fuck all to do with him. When John pressured him for more information, Sully said she was working for Billy, but that was all he knew. John told him he wanted Veronica's address by the following weekend. Within a couple of days, Sully called with an address but didn't have a phone number.

Cormac said the pair of them were crazy but was fearful for Sean, so agreed to drive them down. The day was set for the following Tuesday. Forever the businessman Cormac thought they could do a shift nearby and he'd have a snoop around the area. John told him to fuck off, they weren't going to do a shift, Cormac relented.

There was an atmosphere in the Finn's house, an

111

energy, John was in and out like a fiddler's elbow, he was relishing the task in hand. He was the type of character that was excited by risk. Ma questioned him, asking if he knew what was going on? She wasn't relieved by his explanation that they were about to "Do God's work." She asked Sean what did John mean, God's work?

Sean laughed. "He's just winding you up."

Tuesday arrived. They were setting off later than expected, Cormac had had a broken pinning machine at the workshop that he had to fix. Excited, Sean couldn't wait any longer so knocked John's door and waited in the van. John came out carrying a black holdall, which he flung behind the van seats before jumping in to join Sean. A couple of minutes later, Cormac joined them, Ma waved them off. The roads were quiet, and in fifteen minutes they were on the edge of the city. They pulled into a service station for petrol. Sean and John went to buy sweets and drinks while Cormac filled the tank.

A few miles down the road, Cormac mentioned that Sully had rung him that morning.

John glanced across. "You didn't tell Sully we were going down did you?"

Cormac gave him a look of disgust, "I didn't tell him anything."

John smiled and shovelled a handful of M&Ms into his mouth.

"Did he ask when we were going?" Sean looked over.

"Nah, Sully knows the score, the less he knows the better for him." Cormac replied.

Approaching the M1, John pulled out the holdall he had thrown in earlier. From it, took out a bundle wrapped in a gingham tea towel, he unwrapped it slowly as Sean looked on, inside was a gun. It looked like something left over from the First World War, dull grey, with a wooden grip handle. He checked out both windows before lifting it up for his friends to see.

"Fucking hell, what have you got there?" asked Cormac

THE PICTURE GAME

as he struggled to keep his eyes on the road.

John smiled and placed it on his lap. "I won't use it." He turned over in his hand, "Nice, eh?"

"Are there bullets in it?" asked Sean.

John passed the gun across to Sean, "Nah, but I've got some." He pulled out of the bag a small leather pouch, containing probably eight to ten bullets.

Cormac glanced between his mirrors, the road and the gun. "Put it away, someone's coming up behind us."

A small white van pulled alongside. The driver was wearing a dark uniform. John mumbled under his breath, placing the bag and the gun on the floor. Once alongside, the driver glanced across, and quickly returned his eyes to the road. Cormac maintained his speed, not wanting to appear panicked. They burst out laughing as the van cruised by. On its side read 'A.J. Pest Control, Removal and Prevention'.

"Fucking hell!" Sean called out.

"Listen, keep it in the bag, I'll pull in at Milton Keynes," said Cormac. He didn't like the idea of a gun. But he was excited, and knew better to engage John in any form of dispute.

As they drove, Sean formed a plan. John was to knock the door asking for Veronica, as he was the least known to her. He would say that his mate sent him over, simple as that. If she were a hooker, she'd get that, and invite him in. If someone else answered, he would ask for her and go from there. John could see a problem. Hookers never used their real name, so straight away would be suspicious.

"Best if I say Sully sent me, she fucking knows me anyway," said John.

Cormac said he'd promised not to mention Sully's name.

John disagreed, "Fuck Sully, I'll say that he told me to drop off some gear, only for her. I'll try and get her to the van. Then it's over to you two cunts," he laughed.

Twenty minutes later, Cormac indicated, taking the turn

113

off for the services. He followed the road up and chose an isolated spot in the car park.

"Not here, mate. We'll stand out like a sore thumb, get a bit closer," said John.

Cormac parked behind a dark blue Ford Sierra and kept the engine running.

"You go for a piss," John said to Sean as he opened the door.

Sean looked confused, then the penny dropped and off he wandered, maintaining the ruse. Cormac and John were casually taking in their surroundings, trying to appear as natural as possible. John pulled up the bag onto his lap, taking out the gun.

"Have you used it? Cormac asked. Do you know how to shoot?"

John looked surprised, "It's a fucking gun. I'm not a sniper, but if someone's in front of me and I pull the trigger, they get shot."

They hit the north circular just before midday and were in Hammersmith within a half an hour. Sean was giving instructions from an old A to Z. They pulled into a long, quiet road, the houses were grand, three and four stories high, most had been converted into flats. They scanned the numbers, they were looking for number 289. Realising they'd started at the lower end of the road, Cormac sped up until they hit the 200s.

"221, 239, 251," Sean counted.

They pulled in past 289, parking a few houses down on the opposite side. Cormac leant forward, looking at his brother and friend. Both smiled, Sean nervously, John with excitement.

"Let's sit for a minute," said Cormac.

John called out, "Is that her?"

Veronica had stepped out of her front door and was walking down the pathway.

Sean called, "That's her, that's her!"

"What do you want to do?" Cormac asked him, adding

THE PICTURE GAME

"Grab her now."

Sean was like a rabbit in headlights. He leant over John for the door handle before hesitating.

"What do you mean, grab her, kidnap her, you mean?" Sean replied.

"No, you daft fuck, just speak to her," said Cormac.

Veronica was now walking away, heading up the road. She wore a very distinctive long red woollen cardigan, almost down to the floor.

Cormac started the engine and began to follow. "You better make your mind up. I'm not gonna play gangsters so you can decide if you want to speak to her or not."

"Fuck off," Sean responded. "Pull up alongside her," he was panicking, unsure of himself.

Cormac had now turned the vehicle around.

"Blast the horn, blast the horn!" shouted Sean.

Cormac looked at his brother, wishing he had never agreed to take part.

"Blast the fucking horn!" screamed Sean.

Cormac let out a couple of sharp toots.

Veronica glanced over her shoulder. Seeing the van, she thought she was being pursued by leery builders and walked on, head down.

Cormac blasted again and pulled up to the kerb.

"Hey, Veronica," Sean called out.

There was a stutter in her step, she looked up, taking a few more steps before turning. Sean was leaning over his brother, hanging out of the window.

Her face lit up. "Sean?" she said, "Sean?"

"Yeah, it's me," Sean exclaimed. "How are you?"

The chance encounter had taken them all by surprise.

She didn't answer the question, confused she asked, "What are you doing down here?"

Cormac cut in, explaining that they were delivering in Lambeth and Sean had got them lost. Veronica did not question the story or the chances of them bumping into her.

115

"Where are you off to?" asked Sean.

Now relaxed, she smiled, "Fucking hell, what are the odds." Her voice went up, repeating "What are the odds?"

"Where you off to?" Sean asked.

She raised her hand to her mouth, "I don't believe it. Now that is weird. I was just thinking about you this morning."

Sean grinned, beaming with delight.

Veronica looked at her watch, "Oh fuck, I'm just off to see a friend," panic in her voice, "I've gotta go." She took a step, then turned back, "How long are you guys here for?"

"A few hours, maybe we could meet for a drink before we head home?" Cormac suggested.

Veronica checked her watch again and glanced down the road. "Listen, there's a pub, go down here, turn left at the end of the run, The Peacock. If you're still there around, say, three o'clock, I could meet you there. But I've got to go now." To emphasise the point, she tapped at her watch. "I've gotta go."

"Where you going?" Cormac shouted as she made her exit.

She turned around with a grin and slapped her forehead. "Oh yeah, you can drop me at the Tube."

John got out and Veronica squeezed in next to Sean. With Sean still dumbfounded and John was never one to speak much anyway, the conversation was left to Veronica and Cormac, who asked how long she'd been at the flat. Veronica said she'd moved in in April, but was moving into a flat in the West End, hopefully soon.

"That's gotta be expensive," said Cormac.

"I got a friend Sammy whose got connections in property and is sorting it for me," replied Veronica.

They pulled up at the tube station. Cormac ran through a bogus itinerary to Veronica saying they would be at the pub around three. Veronica gave Sean a friendly kiss before hopping out the van.

THE PICTURE GAME

The love venom squeezed another drop into Sean's veins, "Who the bloody hell's Sammy, pimp or punter?"

17
Sandwich or Baguette

They drove around the corner to a café, it had a French name, Chez something or other, it looked lovely, painted a blue grey colour with tables outside. A young girl came over with the menus.

"We don't need a menu love; do you do sausage sandwiches?" asked Cormac.

"Sure, do you want it as a sandwich?" she asked, pencil and pad at the ready, adding, "We do baguettes too."

Cormac sat up in his seat to look over the menu as the waitress waited, the sandwich was cheaper.

"Look at the white Paki, trying to save himself a few pence." said John laughing.

"It's only fifty pence dearer," said the waitress, tilting her head.

Cormac smiled at John and chose the baguette with tea, Sean too.

John was trying to lose a few pounds so stuck with a drink, giving a quiet "Phwoar," as he watched the waitress disappeared inside.

They sat smoking as they waited for their order.

Sean spoke up saying he was sure now, Veronica's connection Sammy, was probably an Arab, a pimp.

John agreed, saying Arabs had names like that, "Sammy, Bobby, Harry, made up fucking English names."

Cormac was not so sure, he argued that it could have been Samantha. "And even if it were a Sammy, it didn't

THE PICTURE GAME

mean she was working for, or fucking him."

The other two were unconvinced.

The food was served with an accompaniment of salad and a few crisps, which looked impressive.

"You wouldn't get that in Cov'," John remarked, pinching a few of the crisps.

"You can have the lettuce," laughed Sean.

It didn't take them long to finish off their food. They left and drove further in, parking close Sloane Square. John stuffed the gun below his seat, pushing it in as tightly as he could.

The Kings Rd was busy with tourists checking out the latest styles. A pair of outrageously dressed queens walked arm in arm towards them, Cormac straightened himself up. One of the queens noticed, smiled and blew him a kiss as they passed.

"Hey, he just blew you a kiss," said Sean, nudging his brother.

Cormac laughed and pretending not to have noticed but glanced over his shoulder, receiving another kiss on the breeze for his efforts. They wandered around looking at the shops and bought ice creams. It was still early, they needed to kill a bit more time and found a pub, which was busy with a bustle of lunch-time drinkers. As was usual, Cormac ordered the round, asking for three pints of lager and was surprise when the barmaid asked which one, he chose the cheapest.

A group at the bar were having some sort of party, maybe a dozen men with a tall blonde woman, all in business suits. One of them, a fat guy, was attempting to limbo under the tall woman's arm, with a full pint balanced on his head.

"That fat cunt ain't gonna get under there," sniggered John. But was surprised as the man dipped below with ease, and lifted the glass from his forehead, to the cheers of his friends. "Fucking hell, there you go, you never know." John said clapping.

119

THE PICTURE GAME

The fat man looked over and raised his pint.

They found an empty booth away from the din. On the walls were photos of film and rock stars. The boys had fun trying to name as many as they could. Elvis's Viva Las Vegas was playing on the jukebox. A man in pinstriped was taking song orders from his friends, queuing up the records.

John laughed as he went through their plan to storm Veronica's flat, all guns blazing. He swore he would be up for it, which he was.

Sean wasn't really listening, his spirit was floating in the clouds, heading out towards the heavens. He'd downed his pint, whilst the other were barely halfway down theirs and with nervous energy was blabbering to no one in particular.

Cormac told him to quieten down as he nervously looked around. Slightly offended, Sean stood to get the round in. John by now was feeling hungry and asked for a bag of peanuts, searching through his pockets for a few extra pence to pay for them.

"No don't worry, I'll sort it," said Sean as he wandered off.

"What the fucks come over him?" John asked Cormac.

Shaking his head, Cormac bit down on his lip, "I don't know, but she's fucked him up good and proper." He took a drink, "Do you think it's because she's Sully's bird?"

John shrugged.

Cormac went on, "I reckon it is, but like Sully said, she don't give a fuck. He ain't used to that. What's that saying about unrequited love?"

John was unsure, "What?"

Getting his quotes confused Cormac went on, "The love that cannot call its name."

"You mean pussy whipped," said John.

Cormac laughed, "Yeah!"

As Sean waited to be served, John sidled in beside him and chatted to the limbo party. The fat guy's name was

THE PICTURE GAME

Richard, who said they were celebrating their monthly bonus. John had never heard of a monthly bonus, and made a point to mention it to Cormac later.

"One for yourself," Sean said to the barmaid as she took his money.

"Fucking hell mate, you alright?" John laughing at Sean's generosity.

Cormac nodded as he passed them on his way to the toilet. The toilet walls were a splendour, decorated with posters, postcards and beermats, not an inch was spared. One poster was promoting a gay night in Camden. Cormac glanced over his shoulder and moved along the urinal to take a closer look. The door opened on one of the cubicles. Hurriedly, Cormac finished what he was doing and left. The second pint took a bit longer, Sean seemed to have calmed down. It was two o'clock when Cormac checked his watch, he figured it would take about a half-hour to get over to Hammersmith. At twenty-five past, he told the boys to drink up, they downed the rest of their beer and left.

The Peacock was a beautiful timber fronted traditional London pub, lots of polished brass and dark wood. John did the honours as Sean scanned the room for Veronica. There was a smattering of customers, mostly couples, and a few dusty looking builders. Veronica had taken off her cardigan and was sitting with her back to them on a tall stool. She was talking to a blonde girl of about eighteen, hair in a Dusty Springfield beehive style, dark eyeliner licking past her eyes onto her temple. They were in a booth, high bench seats with a round table and stools scattered about.

Sean nudged his brother and nodded towards Veronica, as John passed out the beer. Feeling sure she'd already spotted them, Sean tried playing the carefree lover, but his eyes betrayed him. They stood chatting at the bar for a while heading going over. The girl with the eyeliner, had been watching, and as they approached, she glanced up

121

alerting Veronica, who rose from her seat and embraced each of the boys in turn, introducing them.

"This is my Sean," and planted a kiss on his cheek, "and this is his brother," pausing, "you're Cormac, right?" she giggled.

Cormac nodded.

She continued as though hosting a TV gameshow. "And this is…" a pregnant pause followed before John introduced himself.

The young girl reached out, shaking hands with each in turn.

"And who is this?" asked John excitedly.

"This is Champagne," said Veronica. Once again, the TV hostess.

"Champagne?" said John. "That's…"

"I'm an unusual girl," Champagne replied with a dirty laugh.

Sean asked if he could buy them a drink. Veronica chose a gin and lime. Champagne asked for a glass of champagne, only to laugh with a wave of her hand. "No, I'm joking, just a gin and lime too."

When Sean was at the bar, Champagne shouted, "Champagne, only the best, none of that cheap stuff," teasing.

The barman glanced over at her and back to Sean, who laughed, giving a thumbs up, but ordered gin and limes. He returned with the drinks and sat himself on the stool next to Veronica, listening to the banter. When it seemed as though Champagne had the attention of the boys, he leant in.

"So, what have you been up to?" he asked in barely a whisper.

She frowned, saying she had planned to be in touch but things had been hectic.

Sean had planned to start with small talk but out of his mouth popped, "What's going on with you and Sully, are you working for him?"

THE PICTURE GAME

She eyes him suspiciously, initially saying yes, but after a bit of probing revealed it was Billy. The questioning didn't bother her, she expected as much. "I would have called you. But it's like I said, things have been crazy down here."

Sean thought she was lying, smiling he looked down at the floor. She placed a hand on his knee. he looked up, placing his on top of hers.

Champagne glanced across, "You two having a lover's tiff?"

Veronica took a sideways glance and grinned. After an hour Champagne said she had to meet up with her boyfriend at four and was running late. Veronica agreed to walk with her to the bus stop and asked Sean if he would come too.

"We'll be back in 20 minutes or so," she said, pulling on her cardigan.

The bus pulled up as soon after they arrived. Champagne embraced Veronica with kisses on both cheeks, repeating the 'Au revoir,' with Sean.

Veronica asked if Sean wanted to see her where she lived and as they turned into her road she apologised as began the description. "It's nothing special, walls are all magnolia, don't get too excited," she warned with a laugh. "The landlord won't let 'us' paint them any other colour."

Of course, Sean was not in the slightest bit interested in magnolia walls, it was with carnal intention he climbed the stairs.

She unlocked the front door, the smell of jasmine wafted towards them, it was overpowering. Veronica asked if he liked it?

"Yeah, I love it," he lied.

The hallway was narrow and gloomy, with a coat peg festooned to overflowing. To the right was a small tidy kitchen. Straight ahead was the lounge and on the left a bedroom.

Sean followed her into the kitchen. "Nice," he nodded

in approval.

"This way," she said leading him by the hand through to the lounge.

"Cream, cream, cream," she said, waving her arm up laughing.

The only splash of colour was a Rolling Stones, Sticky Fingers poster above the fireplace.

"Sit down, I'll make us a coffee," she said, returning to the kitchen.

Sean wandered over to the window, he looked up and down the road. A thin faced man was walking a greyhound on the other side, he glanced up and caught Sean's eye and winked.

"Fucking hell, I bet he's been here," Sean thought, the love sick poison doing its work. He heard the kettle click and the sound of water running as she washed out the mugs.

"Sugar?" Veronica shouted.

"Two please," he called back.

She appeared smiling, mugs in hand. They sat on a purple velour couch, and drank in silence. Eventually, Sean spoke up.

"You into the Stones?" looking up at the poster.

"Nah, Sully gave it me," she replied, with a wry smile.

Again, silence.

"Nice coffee," Sean said, lifting his mug into the air.

Veronica spluttered with her hic-upy laugh, coffee coming down her nose. She grabbed a tissue from her bag and placed her cup on the coffee table.

"What?" he said, not sure what had caused her outburst.

Waving a no, she took a few gulps of air. "You make me laugh."

Sean asked again, "What?"

"Nothing, nothing," she said, trying to pull a straight face. Sean lunged forward embracing her. She giggled as they wrestled, pinching and tickling each other. Once face to face, there was an unconscious pause as they gazed at

THE PICTURE GAME

one another. They kissed passionately and were naked in seconds.

Slowly they explored each other, gentle caresses, as might a collector, touching, feeling, holding back and admiring. Veronica led him through to the bedroom, and onto the bed. Their lovemaking was quick, both already on the edge of ecstasy. Once satisfied they lay in that dreamlike trance that love bestows. Just as sleep was about to take them, Veronica stirred.

"We'd better get back. They'll think I've kidnapped you."

"Fuck 'em," came Sean's reply, though he was already raising himself up.

Veronica left the bedroom to wash and straighten herself out. Sean wandered back into the lounge and quickly dressed. As he was waiting, like a thief, he looked around. He found a notepad, extracts of poems, or song lyrics. Her bag was at the side of the couch. He bent down and unzipped it, the bathroom door opened, he quickly closed it again.

"Do you need to wash your cock?" she asked, without a hint of embarrassment.

Sean looked down to his fly, washing after sex wasn't something he usually did but nodded and wandered off. He ran the tap and washed himself. Not wanting to dry his knob on a towel, he looked around for something and rolled off some toilet tissue, dabbing himself dry. With the curiosity of the obsessed he checked her bathroom cabinet. Then her washing basket. A green and white vanity bag lay by the side of the bath. Turning on the tap to cover his actions, he unzipped it. Rifling through the cosmetics, he found a collection of condoms, maybe a dozen. He stood for a moment, his heart sunk. Picking one up he sniffed the packet and placed it back, covering them over once more.

They walked arm in arm, Sean was confused, at the same time as Cupid was whispering sweet nothings, the god of jealously was shouting bitter somethings.

125

Before entering the pub, Veronica stopped and faced Sean, "You ok?"

"Yeah I'm fine," Sean replied, smiling to hide vulnerability.

She thought for a moment, "Hey, why don't you come down for a visit."

Cupid hit a bullseye, as Sean's heart leapt. "That would be great."

She gazed at him, taking in his vulnerability, "This weekend?" she suggested.

He paused but his eyes lit up, "Yeah I can do this weekend."

Veronica played with him, "Hold on, ah, no I can't do this weekend, this weekend is no good me," she lied, "Why not the following one?"

Sean hesitated, his emotion on a stop start, "*Yeaah,* I can do that."

Veronica smiled.

They entered to a cheer from Cormac and John, both pointing at their empty glasses. Sean asked Veronica what she wanted to drink and called out to the other two. The pub had filled up, Veronica knew a few of guys at the bar, who she said hello to before sitting down.

The conversation turned to what Veronica did on her fashion shoots. She said it was boring, most of the time sitting around as they set up a scene. The photographers were David Bailey wannabees. Some of the other girls were ok, others were up themselves, mostly posh tarts, the male models were usually gay. Cormac asked if she did the catwalk, like the fashion shows on the telly. Veronica explained that catwalk models and photographic models were different. A lot of photographic models couldn't do catwalk, years ago, she did it but was now not young and skinny enough.

"What, you're too fat?" John could not believe it, he looked her up and down incredulously.

"For catwalk, yeah," Veronica shrugged. "You gotta be

THE PICTURE GAME

under seventeen and as skinny as a stick."

She paused to take a look at each of their hands and suggested that Cormac could do hand modelling, but not Sean whose fingers and nails were all bitten and John's wonky knuckles were a definite no-no.

"Ha, ha," said Cormac, nice to know I could earn a few quid with these suckers," he waved his hands.

"What does Billy have to do with it? asked Sean.

"Billy knows everybody," she rolled her eyes, "He can always get you work. Sometimes I'm just handing out leaflets. Modelling ain't what it's cracked up to be."

"So why are you doing it?" Sean said, his tone sharp.

"Better than knocking doors trying to sell pictures," she said testily. "Fuck off, why do you do your job?"

As it was heading into the evening, Cormac suggested they better make a move. At the van, Sean kissed Veronica, she said she'd call him and wrote his phone number on the back of her hand. Cormac said he'd drop Veronica off but she said she'd be fine it was only a five-minute walk.

By the time they hit the M1 Sean was fast asleep, head nudging the window. John and Cormac lowered their voices as they discussed Veronica.

"I can understand why she's got under his skin. She's got something about her, fucking beautiful too," said John. "Do you reckon she's on the game?"

Cormac put his foot down as he was overtaking a truck, checking his mirrors, he pulled back into the inside lane. "I don't know." He changed into fifth gear, pulling into the inside lane and settled into a steady sixty, "You know what I think, she does model, probably meet some guy and if she likes him, she'll fuck him. And then, a few gifts later, she'll fuck him again, you know what I mean." He went on, "If she's paying for that flat, it'll cost her a packet, and if she moves into the West End, fucking hell." He blew out a breath.

John sat considering his friend's thoughts and glanced

127

towards the now snoring Sean. Cormac looked back and forth, waiting for John to respond, instead John folded his arms across his chest, the alcohol providing a pillow on which he closed his eyes.

Cormac opened the window, taking deep gulps down through his lungs and turned up the radio.

An hour and a half later, they pulled in at the workshop. Sean awoke, yawning and stretching. A shudder went through John's body, who took a deep breath and rubbed his face. The workshop was deserted, Cormac wanted to see the day's progress and double check everything was locked up properly. The boys watched from the van as like an old time policeman, he did his rounds.

18
Cruel Cruel Heart

It was a Wednesday morning and word had gotten around about Veronica when Sue phoned. She said she was calling around to sort things out. Sean said he had to go out and was going to be busy all day, she said she was coming anyway.

There was a knock on the door Ma answered, she knew the score with Sean and his girlfriends and although didn't like the idea would lie for him.

"Hello love, you've just missed him, can I give him a message?"

Sue was in a terrible state, her eyes were bloated and cheeks raw from wiping away her tears.

Ma was in a quandary, she was not a fan of the girls on the pictures, never the less, her heart went out to the pitiful figure in front of her. She took a step forward and whispered, "Maybe it was best if you forget about Sean," and smiled. "You're a beautiful looking girl, I'm sure there's plenty of other lads who would queue up to take you out, don't waste your time," Ma raised her eyes to the upstairs window, knowing Sean was watching.

Sue looked up, just as Sean ducked back.

Sue handed over a letter which Ma promised to give to Sean.

By the time Ma had closed the door, Sean was in the hall just out of sight.

"What did she say?" he asked.

THE PICTURE GAME

"If you wanted to know you should have answered the door," Ma replied. "Here, take this," she handed him the letter. "Your being cruel to that girl, you need to let her know if you're not interested."

With the sadistic grin of the ignoble he took the letter upstairs to wallow in his cruel strength. He read as Sue poured out her tender heart, dried tears splashed on the paper, pleading for Sean to meet up, maybe they could sort things out? It was signed, 'All my love Sue.' Sean had no intention of responding, he was a coward at heart, but knew he could only hide for so long.

"Let her know," Ma called up to him.

It was the following week, Sean had not been out on a shift for a while and knowing Sue would be working today, it was time to face the music. He was just finishing off pie and chips when a blast of a car horn rang out.

"That's the lads for you," said Ma getting to her feet.

John had been top seller so was sitting in the front seat, Sue was sitting behind him. On seeing Sean, her face lit up, he ignored her and jumped in.

Ma went over and made a point of saying a few words to Sue and waved them off. She wondered how things would work out and hoped Sean would do the decent thing. She looked up at the sky, the sun was shining, with a bit of luck she might be able to get a wash on the line, she thought.

Sue tried to coax then flirt but with no reaction, she folded her arms and fumbled for a tissue. Sean glanced over, she caught him, she tried a smile, he looked away. Dejected, she asked John if he'd mind going in the back. John was sensitive enough to understand. Stan stopped the car and they swapped places. The atmosphere was uneasy. Sue sat arms folded defensively. John shook his head and smiled across at Sean, who pulled a face.

"Put the radio on," Sean called out.

It was Steve Wright in the Afternoon, their favourite radio show.

THE PICTURE GAME

"Turn it up," Sean asked.

Steve was doing an impression of Mick Jagger, one of his best characters.

"He does him great," said Stan.

At the outskirts of Coventry, Stan pulled in for petrol. John went to the shop, giving Sue and Sean a bit of time on their own. Sue turned sharply to Sean, who smiled smugly back, she straightened to face the front.

Sean paused, before asking, "What's the matter with you?"

She didn't acknowledge him.

He tapped her shoulder, repeating, "What's the matter with you?"

She responded, "You know damn well."

Sean sat back in his seat, shaking his head and let out a huff.

Steve Wright was now chatting and laughing with one of his guests.

Sean fidgeted with the back of the driver's seat before raising his voice, "What do I know?"

Sue looked towards him, her eyes pleading.

He leant forward, head pressed against the front seat, "You knew what the score was between us, you knew."

She sat in stoic silence.

Stan and John were sharing a joke as they crossed the yard. John jumped in, with Stan edging into his seat with his usual oohs and aahs.

"Stan," said Sue. "Would you do me a big favour?"

He looked across at her, eyes red, her cheeks wet with tears. "What?" Stan asked.

"Would you take me home?"

Stan paused for a moment, before looking over his shoulder at the boys in the back. Both shrugged their shoulders. He opened the glovebox and pushed in the petrol receipt and closed it.

"Please," she pleaded, her mouth had turned down as she gulped back a cry.

Stan let out a breath, glancing back to Sean and John. "I better get her home."

"Whatever, mate," said Sean abruptly, adding, "Fucking wasting our time."

Stan started up the car.

They drove like a funeral procession, sombre and quiet, Stan's eyes fixed on the road, while the others stared blankly out of the windows.

Halfway along, Sean shouted out, "Why did you come out? I didn't want you here!"

Sue didn't respond, her self-respect intact.

"Fucking bitch," he muttered, not clearly audible but they all knew what he said.

Hey, watch yourself," said John.

Sean repeated the curse, quieter this time. John glanced over, his expression saying calm down. They pulled into Sue's road. Smart bungalows lined each side, clean, modern, and fresh. They stopped at number fifty-two.

Sue got her stuff together, opened the door and got out, before leaving she leant back into the car.

"Thanks, Stan," she waited, not looking at the two in the back. "I don't think I'll be doing this anymore."

Stan and John smiled at her, Sean glared out of the window on the other side.

Pausing, she added, "Stan if you want to go out for a drink or whatever, you've got my number."

She turned, striding boldly up her pathway, opened her front door and disappeared inside.

Stan sat, jaw on his lap, unable to take in what had just happened. John was rolling with laughter, Sean too but his laugh was hollow and empty.

"How could she?" he thought. "Stan, fucking hell, Stan the man. That's a joke, surely?"

"She's fucked you good, man." John was in hysterics.

Stan looked across in disbelief.

"Are you gonna ring her?" asked John, glancing at Sean as he spoke.

THE PICTURE GAME

"Fucking right I am," Stan cackled.

19
Love and Hate

Later that same evening, Sean arrived at the workshop, it had taken him twenty minutes to walk up from home. Cormac was on his own fixing the stapling machine and had stripped it down. One of the small springs had broken. It was a regular occurrence, so he had spares.

Sean wanted to tell him about the incident with Sue. As he spoke the smell of stale beer hit Cormac every time Sean opened his mouth. Annoyed, he looked up, same old story he thought, Sean and his fucking women, week in week out.

Cormac had other concerns on his mind, new teams were setting up weekly, business was getting tight. Sellers were saying that the whole country had been hammered. Only yesterday, one team complained that having driven all the way to Wales, only for doors to have been knocked the previous night. Generally he ignored complaints from sellers, these were the same guys spending like footballers wives once they struck a lucky vein. But this was happening all the time now. Good sellers were not bringing home the money and switching teams like musical chairs.

"What did you expect her to say?" said Cormac. "You need to start thinking about other people. It's always just about you."

Sean walked away. He could see his brother was in a bad mood. Better to leave him to the stapler repair, he

THE PICTURE GAME

thought. He wandered around the worktable, picking up stray pins, putting them into a box. Cormac's eyes followed him, Sean's cheery smile was returned with a scowl.

Sitting on top of the table he looked around for something to play with. He picked up a stack of backboards, small cardboard sheets which supported the print in its frame. He placed one on the edge of the table, flipping it like a beer mat. It hit the floor. Picking it up, he tried again. It hit the floor a second time.

Cormac shouted, "Can you fuck off, you're annoying me now!"

Sean ignored him and continued flipping the board. This time, as it flew, he managed to snatch it, shouting out "One," in celebration.

Cormac glared over, shaking his head.

Sean was enjoying provoking his brother. He continued and with every success, would shout out a number.

"I'm aiming for ten." The next few got him to seven, but for whatever reason, he could not budge further. "This board's fucked," He pulled off another, but that didn't help. He was stuck on seven. He tried the first board again. Distracted, he had not noticed his brother creeping up on him.

Forcefully Cormac snatched the boards, placing them back onto the pile. Sean grabbed trying to pull one back. They tussled, Sean pulling at the complete pile, flinging them off the shelf. They hit the floor with a thud. Cormac leant down, picking up a couple of pieces. The corners had collapsed. Still squatting, he flicked through the rest. The majority were in the same condition. They cost pennies, but as is often the case, pennies start wars.

"You've fucked them up," Cormac looked up.

Sean stood defiantly.

"You've fucked them up," Cormac repeated, now facing his brother.

Sean dipped into his pockets and pulled out a crisp

THE PICTURE GAME

fiver. With both hands, he pushed it into Cormac face, rubbing it into his nose. "There, you tight arsed cunt. Go put an order in."

Cormac sneered and with a twist of his hips, slammed his fist towards his brother's face, it caught him on the neck but sent Sean sprawling on his backside. Sean rubbed the back of his hand across his lips and tasted blood. Cormac was looming, face contorted, with the eyes of a demon. Sean tried to sit up but as he did, Cormac stepped in, not allowing him to rise. Sean grabbed Cormac's legs, who toppled on top of him. Fists, knees, elbows and heads fought their separate battles. Cormac tried to support his front quarter, but Sean hit him a blow to the side of the face, knocking him sideways. Cormac repositioned himself only to be hit with another stinging blow to the same side of his face. It was evident that Cormac was stronger, but Sean was quicker. Sean had twisted in Cormac's grip and now had his back to his brother. Panting, Cormac took control, with a predators delight. Another blow, this time full force to the side of his Sean's face. The violence and closeness aroused Cormac. With his arm across Sean's throat, he squeezed, feeling the panic and fear beneath him. Sean's elbow hit him, but it did not land with any force. Sean tried to grab at Cormac's face, managing to get his fingers into his hair but with the pressure on his neck, he was losing consciousness. Leaning forward, Cormac could feel his brother's hair, he pressed his lips against Sean, tasting the struggle. Excited, Cormac now had a hardon bulging in his pants. He was on the edge of release. In a moment it was over, his head filled with an explosion of ecstasy. With breath after breath, he slowly released his grip. Sean slumped forward. Cormac's eyes were now half-closed, he was on all fours and could still smell his brother's fear. With the demon released, he eased himself up and disappeared into the toilet.

Sean sat looking down at his jeans and wiped away the

THE PICTURE GAME

blood and snot with the back of his sleeve. Cormac reappeared with a damp cloth and pulled his, bloodied and abused brother, back to his feet. Sean was unaware of what had happened. To him, it was just another dust-up. One of many he had with Cormac. He took the cloth and went to the toilet to see the damage. His face was red and bruised but not yet swollen. There was blood on his lip and still more dripping from his nose. Apart from a few scratches, there were no real marks on his neck. Tenderly he pinched the bridge of his nose, holding it for a minute with his head tilted backwards. He checked the mirror, it still looked straight, hopefully it wasn't broken. His jeans were bloodstained, for some reason only one leg had taken the brunt of the damage. Filling the sink with water, he worked with the cloth, managing to at least dilute, if not clean the marks.

Not wanting to go back into the workshop, he sat down on the toilet. Fear had loosened his bowels, he flushed and cleaned himself. Back at the mirror, he wondered what Veronica would think and wished that he wasn't going down at the weekend. A crimson drip hit the white of the sink. He wiped it with his hands, and made two small plugs of tissue paper, sticking one in each nostril.

Cormac had tidied up the pile of backboards and was now finishing off the stapler repair, putting the few final screws in the cover. He looked around aimlessly as he waited for Sean to reappear, impatiently he knocked toilet door. "You okay?"

There was a pause before the door opened, Sean appeared. "Yeah fine."

Cormac tenderly touched his brother's eyebrow. "You sure?" adding, "I'm sorry, I'm really sorry." He leant in and tenderly kissed Sean's forehead. "I've got a lot on," head bowed in contrition.

"Yeah, well you didn't have to take it out on me, cunt." reacted Sean, wiping the kiss from his face.

A spark reignited, Cormac snarled, "Don't start again."

"Do not fucking start," he glared and pressed his face close.

They stood nose to nose, staring intently for ten seconds or so. Sean dropped his gaze. Cormac continued for a second or two more, underlining his dominance.

Ma was furious and had to be held back by Sean as she heard the rudiments of the incident. Sean initially suggested that he had caught his face on the corner of the workbench, but Ma could sense the icy atmosphere between the two. After a lot of shouting, Cormac disappeared upstairs.

Bewildered Ma ordered Sean to lie on the couch and covered his face with a pack of frozen peas wrapped in a tea towel. The swelling had developed, both eyes were partly shut and his nose had broadened with bruising. Sean's once fine features were raw and bloated. Ma stripped off his jeans and washed them.

As she scrubbed, she talked to herself. anger and rage, whispered in her ear. She was to be judge, jury and executioner. Biting hard down on her lower lip, she vowed to make Cormac pay. But Ma was a Kelly, it was in her blood, a flicker would turn into a raging flame, only to die away by nightfall. Once she had hung out the jeans, calm had descended, she went upstairs to check on Cormac.

Cormac recognised the slow steady steps and sat upright, waiting for her to enter. Cautiously she knocked, this was unusual, as knocking was not a precaution she usually adhered to. Cormac did what was expected and invited her in. She stood, hands on hips, looking at her eldest son, he looked contrite and nervous. She frowned and sat down on Sean's bed, facing him.

"What happened?" she enquired, voice soothing, head to one side.

Cormac let out a breath, "You know what he's like. He was trying to get me going," he looked over to his mother.

Ma waited slowly nodding, allowing the silence to develop until Cormac went on.

THE PICTURE GAME

"He was throwing around the stock," he said, adding, "He's fallen out with one of the girls that… works for us. And he wanted to take it out on me."

He was making a good fist of his argument, very much in his favour.

Ma's eyes narrowed, "Which girl?"

"Sue. One of the girls on the shift," Cormac replied.

"That girl that was here the other day? There must have been something in that letter that's upset him." Ma shook her head, "The wee hoo'r, and she seemed such a nice girl." Immediately, she relaxed, standing she straightened herself, thinking, "That'll be it alright, sluts most of them, certainly not decent girls." Then to Cormac, "Ah, he'll be over her in a week or so, if I know that lad well, keep an eye on him will you son."

"I will Ma," said Cormac.

20
Down the Smoke

Coventry bus station, Pool Meadow, was a mile walk into town. Sean arrived fifteen minutes early. Already passengers were waiting, some with suitcases, some with bags, whilst others travelled light. Sean was wearing an army jacket over his jeans, he'd an ex-army luggage canvas sack, he looked cool.

A West Indian family stood alongside him, a man, his wife and five children. The father was a man of about forty, lean, tall and straight, who took one look at Sean's bruised face and kept his distance. In contrast his wife was warm and friendly, chatting to Sean as she nursed her youngest. The bus arrived, the queue moved forward as passengers got off. The driver rose from his cabin waving the first passenger off the platform, locked the bus and disappeared. Moans and groans filtered down the queue as everyone settled back.

"Why didn't he let us on?" said the West Indian lady with a huff.

Sean shrugged his shoulders, letting out a breath of frustration. Five minutes later, a different driver arrived, far more cheerful than his colleague, fresh and ready for work.

"All aboard for the Magical Mystery Tour," he called.

With a hiss the pneumatic doors opened.

The West Indian lady and her children clapped, "All aboard," she laughed, herding them towards the front.

THE PICTURE GAME

Sean chose a seat next to the window and played peek-a-boo with a cheeky faced boy in front. But by the time they were on the outskirts of the city, he was regretting starting the game and ignoring the boy he gazed out the window.

The mother, a slim dark haired women, looked over her shoulder, "They wear you out," she offered in sympathy, Sean smiled.

He was familiar with the route; he'd done it hundreds of times before. But from the height of the bus, it was different, he enjoyed watching the cars as they passed below, occasionally making stories in his mind about the passengers.

They arrived in Victoria bang on schedule. He looked at his A to Z map book, checking the Tube stations on the back. Only after speaking to a driver did he realise the Tube was a quarter of a mile up the road.

He bought a weekend ticket and searched for Hammersmith on the tube map. He knew it was on the District line but was anxious to ensure he caught it going in the right direction. The sounds and the rush of the underground took him by surprise, perhaps his senses were heightened. Twenty minutes later, he surfaced into daylight. Looking up at the road signs and the A to Z, he mapped his way to Veronica's flat.

At her gate, he glanced up at her window, hoping she was looking down, she wasn't. He pressed Flat 2, the buzzer sounded, the door clicked open and he went in and up the stairway.

Champagne was standing in the doorway, wearing a red satin robe which finished on her thighs. She seemed to recognise his disappointment. "Don't worry, she'll be back in a bit. Come in, I'll get you a coffee."

"Thanks," he responded.

His mind followed his groin to the pleasures of the flesh, wondering whether he should make a play for Champagne, as her hips sashayed in front of him.

THE PICTURE GAME

"Sit yourself down," she said, waving in the direction of the lounge.

Sean wandered through. She shouted something, something about his journey.

He only caught the tail end and shouted back, "Yeah."

Champagne arrived coffee in hand. "I was asking what time you set off?"

She placed his mug on the table.

"Oh my god, what's happened to your face?" She recoiled and then leant in closer.

Sean felt embarrassed and lowering his head. "A bit of a disagreement with my brother, no big deal."

"What did you disagree about?"

Sean didn't want to go into detail, saying it was a row about work, then changed the subject. "I left Cov' at eight, caught the bus down."

Champagne sensed his discomfort so did not pursue a fuller explanation. "Into Victoria?" she asked, wincing as she covertly checked out his bruises.

"Yeah, fucked about there for a half an hour. I didn't know the tube was up the road."

Champagne laughed and flicked back her hair. She had an attractive, impish manner. "Oh, I did that the first time I came down here." Then added with a smirk, "Even after I was told, I still walked around the block twice."

They both laughed.

Champagne was usually a very gregarious person but like a lot of people when in the company of someone they fancy, she became tongue tied.

They sat in silence for a drawn-out moment, before Sean abruptly asked, "Where are you from?"

A grateful Champagne replied, "Near Birmingham, Kidderminster." She looked to him, "Do you know it?"

Sean shrugged, "Yeah, done it a few times on the pictures.

She went on, "I've been in London now for three years," she took a sip of coffee. "You're from Coventry,

THE PICTURE GAME

Kidderminster," she let out a "Pfaff.... Arse end of the Black Country." She accentuated the town name in a broad Black Country accent and touched his arm. "I was on a fashion course at Dudley College, got an HND, but there's nothing in fashion up there, so the bright lights called me." She spread her palms around her face. "I worked at Selfridges," she looked over, "Selfridges on Oxford Street, on the shop floor. Sooo' boring, raising her eyes to the ceiling. "One day this tall, elegant man comes in, spends five grand at the drop of a hat, just like that!" her eyes widening.

Sean blew out a whistle.

Champagne nodded, "Five, fucking grand he spent on clothes. Not far off what I was earning for a whole bloody year."

As she was talking, Sean sensed something unfamiliar. Maybe she was a little too feminine, maybe too many gestures. Something about her voice was not quite natural. She took another gulp of coffee and it was clear. Her Adam's apple bobbed up and down with every swallow. He blushed, how could he had missed it, Champagne was a man!

"Well, he handed me his card at the till and introduced himself as Billy. He asks if I would be interested in some work, a hundred a day, minimum. I put my arm through his, and that's the last I saw of the men's department of Selfridges," she beamed at Sean.

At that moment, they both understood.

The sound of a key in the lock distracted her. They both stared at the lounge door waiting for Veronica to enter.

"We're in here," sang Champagne as sounds came from the kitchen.

Veronica appeared, Sean's heart fluttered, but he sat stone still.

Champagne nudged him in the back. "He's playing hard to get," adding, "Oh, and don't ask about the face. "

Veronica hesitated, shook her head and smiled, Sean

THE PICTURE GAME

grinned awkwardly before they embraced and kissed. Champagne sat smiling; her hands clutched to her breast. Veronica asked what happened, only to be given the same explanation about a fallout with Cormac. She placed a kiss on his bruised nose.

They cooked bacon and eggs for lunch, and with no table, they sat with plates on their knees.

Champagne suggested they could do the rounds of Kensington Market, Camden, and the King's Road. It seemed like a good idea. The girls left the room to get ready.

Footsteps tripped along the hall as Veronica re-appeared. She was wearing a cream loose chiffon blouse with a black bra beneath and a pair of cut off denim shorts. She looked breath-taking.

"You look fantastic," said Sean.

Champagne emerged from the bedroom holding two summer dresses, asking pink or yellow? Veronica chose pink, Sean agreed.

The plan was to head north, starting in Camden and finishing off in Kensington, maybe The Goat or Prince of Wales for a few drinks, then hit the West End to a club.

Camden market was swarming with tourists. They wandered past stalls selling everything from antique stuffed fish to the latest fun gadgets, with multitudes in between. At one of the stalls Champagne insisted Sean try on a multi zipped black t-shirt, Sean was unsure, knowing his friends would take the piss. But Champagne was having none of it and haggled the stallholder from fifteen quid, down to a tenner and bought it for him.

"You'll love it a few weeks," she said confidently.

Next, she spotted a red hat with feather plumes for herself. Despite Veronica and Sean swearing it looked great, "No," she said looking at herself in the mirror, and left it behind.

Smells from fried doughnuts, burgers, Chinese and Indian foods, competed as they swam and floated in the

THE PICTURE GAME

air. At a stall selling jeans, the girls took charge and pulled out a few pairs of Levi's for Sean to try on.

"No one wears baggy jeans these days," Veronica said laughing.

Champagne giggled, agreeing.

Sean looked around, true enough, no one else was wearing baggy flares.

A Greek-looking guy showed him to the changing room, a curtain, to try them on. All were too short. The Greek shuffled through a pile until he found a longer pair which fitted Sean perfectly. Again, Champagne did the haggling, saving a fiver, they walked on.

Champagne was now reminiscing about the hat and felt sure that actually, it did suit her, they went back but it was gone. She cursed herself, saying, "Fortune favours the brave."

They took the Tube to Sloane Square and followed the crowds heading up The Kings Road.

"Oh, we've got to go in here," said Champagne.

They stood outside Malcolm McLaren and Vivienne Westwood's shop, SEX, the famous punk clothing store.

Pointing at a t-shirt which looked identical to the one Champagne had just bought him, Sean said, "Fucking hell, that's fifty quid." He went over to the window for a closer look. One of the punks wandered over, he looked dangerous, his hair in a mohawk, nose, ears and lips pierced. His head was angled, as he focused in on Sean's bruises.

"Fuck off," said Sean. "What the fuck's up with you?"

The punk didn't respond, but moved off, staring intently at Veronica and Champagne.

Champagne pushed the leather-clad zombie, sending him stumbling to the ground. "Fuck off you cunt,"

The punk got to his feet, his manner had changed.

"I'm sorry, I didn't mean anything," he said in crisp cultured English. A sheep in wolf's clothing, if ever there was one.

145

THE PICTURE GAME

After a quick look around and the odd, "Who the fuck would wear that?" they were back on the King's Road and up for a drink. They found a pub, The Builders Arms and joined a crowd of rosy face Germans sitting on benches outside.

On seeing the girls, they raised their pints with a "Schonen Tag."

Sean made his way to the bar. He returned a few minutes later carrying the drinks. The men leant forward allowing him to squeeze through.

The tallest German looked like an athlete, probably six foot six, if not taller. He leant back, asking in broken English, "Could you chose please good restaurant, perhaps one we stay close, please?"

Veronica laughed, saying they were not from the area so they couldn't help. The Germans chatted enthusiastically in broken English and insisting on buying drinks for everyone. After three, Veronica said they should head off. The goodbyes took ten minutes, with the girls being kissed and hugged perhaps more than they wanted. One remarked how lucky Sean was to have the company of two beautiful ladies.

Sean raised both thumbs, "Ja!"

They decided to skip Kensington market and went straight to The Goat. The pub was dim with a low ceiling, dark wood panelling throughout. A fat hippy looking guy in a Woodstock t-shirt recognised Veronica as they passed in the doorway, they chatted, as Sean and Champagne went to the bar. In the corner a John Denver look alike was strumming out a ballad, he looked the part, fresh faced and glasses.

Sean stripped off and pulled on his new t-shirt, much to the delight of Champagne, and to a chorus of wolf whistles from onlookers.

After only one drink, the drones of the ballads and the alcohol was sending them to sleep. The Prince of Wales had a jukebox and was a lot livelier.

THE PICTURE GAME

It was about eight o'clock that Billy walked in, along with a thin-faced Asian guy. The Asian looked like Marc Bolan, a mass of corkscrew hair, wearing a thin nylon shirt, which was hanging off one shoulder. On spotting the group, Billy made a beeline.

"Fucking hell! What's happened to your face?" he asked, Sean once again went over his fall out with Cormac.

"You Coventry lads are fucked up," said Billy.

He'd just come from a meeting with a record producer who was interested in signing Phil, the Asian guy, who was now busy passing out free tickets to his next gig at the Halfmoon in Putney.

Sean asked Veronica if she had arranged to meet Billy. She said no, but she'd seen him in The Prince of Wales before. Sean was not convinced it was just too much of a coincidence. Veronica nudged him, showing him a tiny bag filled with white powder, they both disappeared.

"Off for a powder," joked Billy.

A few minutes later they returned, all the livelier.

"I've got some charlie if you want to go upmarket," offered Billy.

"We're good, we're good," replied Veronica.

At eleven-thirty, the question was where to go next.

"I know a good nightclub in The West End, and I can get us in for free," said Billy.

Not the types to check the horse's mouth, they readily agreed. The queue was at least a hundred yards long. The club looked like a cinema, complete with neon lights. Billy went straight to the front, speaking to an enormous black bouncer dressed like a drag queen. Moments later, to jeers from the queue they waltzed straight in. It was both cavernous and claustrophobic, filled with transvestites, new romantics, ageing queens and up and coming gangsters. Sean stood mesmerised by the exotic birds on display.

The group split up with Champagne taking Billy and

147

THE PICTURE GAME

Phil, leading them to the bar. A Diana Ross track was playing, 'Love Hangover', Veronica rushed Sean to the dancefloor. Men were dancing with men, women with women, their movements slow, like a disjointed ballet. No one smiled, but all looked fabulous.

Billy gave him a pill, Veronica took one too, they washed them down with vodka. Once more to the dancefloor, like extras from a Warhol video. From then on, the night was a blur. Sean thought he may have kissed Champagne, or maybe it was someone else. He was certain he'd kissed Billy and Phil too. In the taxi back he remembered singing, The Mountains of Mourne.

"Oh Mary, this London's a wonderful sight, where the people are working by day and by night."

The morning was lazy and foggy-headed, sex was slow and satisfying, allowing them to sleep into the afternoon. Veronica poured a steaming hot bath which they shared. Sean got the short end of the stick, with his back against the taps. At two, they made bacon sandwiches together. At three o'clock, Veronica remembered she'd had promised to meet up with a friend for a couple of hours and couldn't get out of it. Sean asked to come along, but Veronica told him he wouldn't enjoy it. She planted a warm sloppy kiss on his lips and hugged him, promising to be back before six.

Once on his own, he rifled through her belongings, making a point to count the condoms in the bathroom, there was now seven, he wished he'd counted the first time. Tucked under her bed was an old shoebox containing photos. There were some of her modelling in various stages of undress but none nude, he laid them out on her bed and masturbated. There were other photos of friends, some school photos and a few black and white ones of her as a child. One he assumed was a photo of Veronica and her parents. She was probably five or six with an oversized costume. Her mother was a slim blonde girl, extremely attractive in a white bikini. Her father, was a tall athletic

THE PICTURE GAME

black man, wearing jeans but no shirt. They were standing on a beach with their backs to the sea, smiling, ice-creams in hand. Sean found some private letters that upon opening, he folded away with guilt, only to return and read. They were mostly written to her from her grandmother, a few were from a friend called Eddy, these were intimate, they were obviously very much in love at one time, which made Sean feel jealous. After reading them he replaced everything as it was and wandered into the lounge.

He went to the window, strangely the thin man with his greyhound was walking by, once again he glanced up and winked. Sean didn't respond but moved away, it all seemed a bit weird, who the fuck was he?

He turned on the small TV set and fell back on the couch. Columbo was on, the picture was surprisingly good, apart from every now and again an eerie shadow appeared and filtered across the screen. He settled down to watch the episode. The buzzer made him jump, he wondered if it might be Veronica back early or even the thin man. He went to the window, Champagne was looking up, she waved, he waved back and buzzed her in. This time Sean did the honours, making tea for himself and a coffee for Champagne. From the lounge, Champagne called out asking where Veronica was and what time she'd be home.

"Well she left about half an hour ago," Sean called back. "Said she'd be back in a couple of hours, she was meeting a friend, but didn't say who." Sean brought the drinks through. "She didn't want me to come along."

Champagne smiled taking the mug of coffee, "Thank you. Veronica knows a lot of people." She paused, "In fact, she's a star of the scene down here."

Champagne's mother had warned her before she left Kidderminster, "You'll meet lots of friends but very few are true in London."

Champagnes thoughts went to her friends, hundreds,

149

THE PICTURE GAME

boys, girls, rich men, poor men, beggar men and thieves, but only Veronica was true. It was Veronica who'd collected her from hospital and nursed her after she'd been beaten up. It was Veronica she turned to when skint. Perhaps the only true friend she ever had. Veronica had always forgiven her, and would forgive her again as she made her play for Sean.

"Oh, I love Columbo, he's so cool," Champagne said with glee. "He was in a lot of Hollywood movies before this, you know." She was sitting cross-legged, about to light up. "Wasn't he in The Magnificent Seven?" she lit her cigarette. "Alongside Yul Brynner and Steve McQueen." A puff of smoke slipped from the side of her lips. "You don't smoke….do you smoke?" she asked unsure, hand halfway to her bag.

"Now and again, but no," he replied. Sean wasn't sure about her film knowledge but agreed, "Yeah, I think he was."

Champagne looked a bit rougher than the previous day. There were the beginnings of stubble, her sing-song black country accent more pronounced. Champagne recognised his apprehension and smiled, if she was going to have success, she didn't want Sean to have any surprises. Life had taught her that surprises were only nice when well received, and could be painful when not.

"What are you doing later on?" Sean took a drink of his tea.

Champagne, "Is that an offer?," she giggled, "We don't want to make Veronica jealous, but then again?" and winked. She really liked Sean, his boyish face and hillbilly outlook. How could a boy be so pretty without bending a bit, now and again?

Sean laughed awkwardly, not sure how to respond.

Champagne pulled on her cigarette; the smoke danced as she spoke. She tilted her head over, Sean smiled.

She reached over and put her hand to his face. "I think you look good with a bit of bruising, makes you look tough."

Sean moved back, he waited as he collected his thoughts. "Erm, it's not my thing."

"What's not your thing?"

"I don't know," he stuttered, "you know," his raised his hands, palms out, "It's not my thing."

Champagne smiled, "Listen, I'm going to love you and leave you." She rose from the couch, adding, "Hey look."

Columbo was summing up the case for the prosecution.

"Like me, he always gets his man," she pouted with a grin, as she stubbed out her fag, "Gonna have to fly," she kissed, and gently licked Sean's cheek.

"Tell her I called," she called out as she descending the stairs.

Sean watched from the window as she strode confidently up the road, "Fucking hell, this London is a weird place," he thought to himself.

Six o'clock passed, nothing decent was on TV and Sean was getting annoyed. He promised himself that he'd scarper if Veronica didn't turn up by seven. Seven o'clock came and went and so did Sean. On the bus home, he promised to himself that he'd fuck her off.

21
In for a Penny

For the next few weeks, Cormac tried hard just to concentrate on his business. From what he could see he was getting only twenty per cent of his money from the selling side, despite it taking up over fifty per cent of his time. He decided to follow Billy's advice and concentrate on what was making money, the manufacturing.

He called Sean and John in for a meeting, telling them that from now on the teams were their responsibility, they run them and take the profits. Cormac said he wanted to focus on manufacturing which he planned to expand and was looking at new premises up Hillfields.

Both Sean and John liked the sound of running their own teams. John asked if they could hire and fire? Cormac shrugged his shoulders saying they could hire and fire, chose where to hit, and decide how many days they went out. But from now on, they had to buy the pictures and manage their own stock. He would allow them thirty days payment which was better than anyone else he supplied but after thirty days, no money, no stock.

"Where are we gonna store our pictures?" asked Sean.

"You can rent a garage or a container, the lads from Willenhall will sort one out for you, but make sure you get a good lock, a real good one." Adding, "A good one won't be cheap, but I wouldn't trust them fuckers over there. Anyway, that's for you guys to sort." He paused thinking, "I tell you what I'll do. I'll pay for a container for the first month as long as you guys sort it out."

It seemed too good to be true and happy, they shook hands on it. Cormac thought that if he could get them on the hook they would work twice as hard, making sure the other sellers did too. If his maths were correct, he would still get the same money without any of the aggravation. He'd also heard on the grapevine that the taxman had begun sniffing around, chasing PAYE tax for sellers, so putting distance between himself and the teams made sense.

It did the trick, both Sean and John raised their game. Cormac was picking up an extra two hundred quid a week for doing fuck all. He'd also managed to pick up extra orders supplying another three teams.

But despite working like a dog, he could not purge uninvited thoughts from his mind. He was drinking more than usual, stopping off at the pub and getting pissed after work had become the norm. In the pub toilet he would linger in the hope of an encounter. He visited toilets in town for the same reason, all to no avail. Until one day, a middle-aged man approached.

Thickset and muscular, he called himself David. Cormac used the name Steve. There was no romance. They shared a cubicle, Cormac giving, as David held onto the cistern. It was over in a couple of minutes. David left first, telling Cormac to wait a while. Cormac wiped himself with tissue and sat on the toilet. This was what he wanted, so fucking what if he was queer?

A week later, as Sean was checking in his order, he was grabbed him from behind. Sean bucked as Cormac folded both arms around his chest. Cormac felt a surge of power and arousal, as Sean struggled. He raised his arm around Sean's neck and held on tight for a few moments, then released.

"What the fuck's up with you?" Sean shouted, sensing Cormac was getting off on it. "You're a fucking weirdo."

Cormac's eyes were cold, he calmly grinned but in a

THE PICTURE GAME

second, he changed, now light and playful, "I was just fucking about with you," he laughed, "Come on, I was just fucking about!" Then looking at the order, "How many have you got?"

Like a dog that's been kicked, Sean stared, unable to gauge what had gone on but felt afraid. "Just what I ordered," he said as Cormac double checked the count.

"Spot-on," Cormac pulled up a pallet truck.

Between them, they loaded up the boot of the black Ford Granada. Cormac pulled back the empty pallet and watched as his brother left. He made up his mind, he would return to the toilets, that night.

The sun had just gone down when he arrived. He wandered around for a while, but didn't have to wait long. An effete boy, slim with green dyed hair entered. A few seconds later, the boy reappeared at the entrance, they caught each other's eye. Cormac followed him inside, tapping on the door of each cubicle.

When he reached the third, he heard a faint. "Hello."

The boy was delicate, skin white as ivory. Not wasting time on an introduction Cormac kissed him on the lips, pushing his hand down the front of the boy's trousers. The boy moaned, already erect. Cormac turned him around, pulling at his clothing, and entered him. His sighs and moans became louder. With one hand, Cormac covered the boy's mouth and the other went to his throat. Cormac held firm, cracking the boys head against the wall as he struggled, only releasing him once he too was released. They embraced and Cormac went down on him.

His name was Adrian, open and comfortable with his sexuality, a college student. He lived in Leamington having moved down from Manchester. Despite his tender years, he was, without doubt, more experienced in the clandestine life of a gay man than Cormac.

"You like it rough, I don't mind too much as long as it don't get too serious," said Adrian.

Cormac was embarrassed, "I do, I get too worked up,

THE PICTURE GAME

probably end up killing someone one day."

"Don't worry, in Manchester you get a lot of Muscle Mary's, no big deal.

"Fucking hell, Muscle Mary's," said Cormac laughing.

"Yeah, oh you lot down here are so in the closet. I've had guys with my cock up their arse, swearing they're straight," laughed Adrian.

Cormac liked him. They walked up through the empty precinct until they found a Wimpy Bar, Adrian ordered a knickerbocker glory, Cormac opted for tea. Adrian suggested they meet up on Saturday at the Rose and Crown, one of the few openly gay pubs in town. Cormac was afraid he might be spotted, but asked where it was and agreed to meet.

By the time Cormac got home, Ma had gone to bed but had put pie and chips in the oven for him. The dinner was as dry as a bone, but a good dousing of vinegar gave it flavour. With his belly full, he went for an early night and was asleep in minutes.

He woke early and was out of the house by seven. Instead of heading to the workshop, he went to the toilets. Bobbie was a plump Asian guy of about thirty. Cormac smiled when he noticed his wedding ring, Adrian was right. Bobby began complaining when things got rough but Cormac didn't stop until he was finished.

Once at work it was business as usual, another stapler to fix, mouldings and prints to order. At lunch, he wanted to go back to the toilets, but restrained himself until evening. Throughout the week he visited other toilets, four of which provided the service he was looking for. As the weeks passed, he went further afield, trying laybys, parks, visiting Birmingham and Leamington, a smooth-skinned Moroccan from Leicester, who liked it rough, rougher the better, his favourite for now. His cottaging habits were predominantly early evening. Not once did he wear a condom. Well, 'Gays didn't get pregnant, and a dose of the clap wasn't going to kill anyone, he reasoned.'

155

THE PICTURE GAME

22
A trip to the Doctors

With Sean away most of the day, and Cormac no longer at home in the evenings, Ma felt isolated. She cooked now only for herself, chatted to herself and sometimes cried by herself. Never before had she felt so vulnerable. They had always been around. Now her days were long and lonely. Of course, she could chew the cud with Aggie, her sister, or call in to see her cousins Bridie or Kathleen, but her heart yearned for the mischief and fun that only her boys provided.

Recognising her sister's despair, it was Aggie who persuaded her to make an appointment with Dr Davis, her favourite.

The waiting room was dull and silent, metal chairs like leftovers from a works canteen. A little boy shyly flicked through the magazines on the table. Ma smiled remembering a line from Peter Pan, "Oh why can't you remain like this forever." She wanted to touch him, to hold him in her arms.

His mother looked over and as though she could read Ma's thoughts. "Show the lady," she said.

The little boy wriggled as Ma helped him up onto the seat next to her. He'd selected a Women's Own magazine. Ma helped him turn the pages and ran her hand over the top of her head, as he looked at the pictures. The boy pointed at a fluffy bear on the table, Ma leant over to get it.

A metallic voice came over the tannoy. "Mrs Wilson."

THE PICTURE GAME

Mrs Wilson smiled and lifted her little boy, "Say bye bye."

"What's his name?" asked Ma.

"Peter," replied Mrs Wilson, she took her little boys hand and waved goodbye.

The little boy blurted something.

"Bye, bye," Ma called as she watched them disappear.

Her appointment was for eleven thirty, at noon she was called in. Dr Davis was sitting on a buttoned leather chair. He looked up and smiled. "Come in, come in, sit down Mrs Finn," in a strong Scottish accent, his arm invited her onto the chair opposite.

Dr Davis had been at the surgery for donkey's years, way before Ma had moved over to Coventry. In his younger days his face was plump and cheery, now it hung, draped with jowls.

"What can I do for you?" his expression inviting, filled with calm and wisdom.

Ma had rehearsed her words. "Well doctor, I've not been so well," she stuttered.

Dr Davis looked over his glasses with imploring interest, slowly nodding as she went on.

"I think it's me nerves," she swallowed.

The doctor waited, but that was as far as Ma got.

"Let's have a look now then," he said, commencing his routine examination, blood pressure, pulse, testing her lungs listening to her heart and as he did so he spoke soothingly, gently waiting until she was ready. "Was there something that has upset you?

"No doctor."

"And the boys are doing well?"

"Very well doctor."

Finally, when the doctor asked what the boys were doing, did her concerns flood out. Dr Davis sat back down, not speaking. He handed her a tissue as he waited for her tears to fall. Once she had finished, he let out a slow breath, and began.

158

THE PICTURE GAME

"I wish I could say that things will return to the way they were. I would like to say that in years to come they will bring their families around and your heart will feel that joy you are missing." He paused, But that is something I do not know" His tone then lifted, "But the one thing I can say is, that change will come. So, whatever you are feeling today Mrs Finn you will not feel the same tomorrow or the next day, or next week or next year. What nature has in line for us we do not know, but from my experience in seeing people day in day out for the last fifty-five years, is that bad things generally change for the better, that's the way nature plays with us. Share your thoughts with those you love and listen to their concerns and worries, because you won't have to scratch deep to see we are all the same. You, me, my neighbours, your neighbours. Life pulls us through the mud at times and the scented flowers and heathers too. Now I can write out a prescription which might help. If you are feeling that's what you want?"

He raised his pen hovering over the prescription pad and looked across.

"I feel a lot better now doctor," she dabbed her face, "now that I've got it out, but I'll take a prescription just in case." Ma said hesitantly.

Dr Davis smiled as he put pen to paper.

On the way home, she called in to see Aggie, who was a qualified nurse.

Aggie asked how she felt?

Ma said a lot better, praising Dr Davies's wisdom.

Aggie nodded, "He's a lovely doctor." As they waited for the kettle to boil, Aggie looked over Ma's prescription. "Ah, he's given you the Diazepam, that's Valium Mary. They'll do. They'll get you back on your feet again."

They sat together in the sitting room sipping on tea, Aggie rose from her seat. "I've got an apple pie on the go, would you like a slice?"

"Oh, that would be lovely," Ma replied.

THE PICTURE GAME

23
The Bong and Sully

Veronica had not been in touch, and wondering if Sully had heard from her, Sean thought he'd call over. Sully answered his door in his underwear, beer can in hand, eyes sleepy, he seemed chilled. Sean followed him through to the lounge. His manner was soon explained, he'd been smoking from a bong. It was about three feet tall, brass, decorated with Islamic patterns and stood in the middle of the floor. He was thrilled with it, explaining to Sean the mechanics. The principle being that by drawing the smoke through the water, it cooled down the smoke, it was a smoother smoke and healthier, so he said.

"And hey, it looks so fucking cool," Sully laughed out loud.

Sean smiled, agreeing that it did look good and asked if Sully could get him one.

"I'll ask my friend Mr Ali from down the road," Sully responded with a wink.

They sat down Sully offered Sean a draw of the pipe, and laughed as Sean coughed his heart up with his first go. A few more draws and Sean got the hang of it.

It was Sully who brought up the subject of Veronica.

Sean played down his interest, "I saw her a couple of weeks ago, but she fucked off. She left me sitting in her flat, went off somewhere. Said she was seeing a friend.

He waited for a reaction from Sully, who grinned as he sucked down hard on the pipe.

161

THE PICTURE GAME

Sean went on, "I got sick of waiting, so I fucked off."

"Yeah I heard, told you she was fucked up," replied Sully, letting go of a light blue cloud of smoke.

Sean shrugged.

Sully passed the pipe over, put up a finger and coughed, "I spoke to Billy," again he coughed, "she's still working for him."

"What is she doing for Billy anyway?" Sean asked.

"What do you think she does?"

Sean paused, and took another pull on the bong, his heart wanted to say one thing but his head spoke out. "Is she a hooker?" he passed the pipe back.

Sully took couple of long draws, glanced over, nodded and laid back against the couch.

Sean went on, his voice faltered as he swallowed the bitter pill, "I thought she was, she's got a bag full of nodders in her bathroom."

"Doesn't surprise me," said Sully.

"She is a good fuck though," said Sean, laughing to conceal his pain.

"Tell me about it," Sully replied.

They both laughed at that one.

Sully took another pull on the bong and handed the pipe over. "Do you know that bloke or girl she hangs out with?" Sully asked.

"You mean Champagne, yeah?" Sean drew in the smoke deep into his lungs, held it and slowly released it. "I couldn't believe it! Met him in the pub at the end of her road from Veronica's, John tried to get off with him, her, thought it was a bird." Sean made no mention of Champagne's feeble seduction attempt for fear Sully would get suspicious about Sean's sexuality.

Sully laughed, grinning, "She's alright though, ain't she? I'd fuck her, pretend I never saw his cock, Sully laughed. "Real tits!" he laughed again.

Embarrassed, Sean shook his head unsure what to say.

Sully coughed, raised his hand in the air and slapped

162

his chest, another cough. "He's a decent guy, but even more fucked up than Veronica. He knocked the shit out of her once. I heard his dad fucked him when he was fourteen. What a cunt, that's gonna fuck with you ain't it?"

"Fucking hell…. that's fucked up," said Sean, his face twisted with disgust.

Sully shook his head and waited, considering, before going on. He took another long draw on the pipe. "A lot of queers are schizo, I guess it's all the shit they have to take." He leant back, his movements slower now, his speech barely a whisper, he blew out the smoke, "Yeah, it's a hard life."

24
The Ports of Amsterdam

Holland was a rare treat for a picture seller, profitable and fun. The Dutch were loaded, spoke great English, with a free and easy lifestyle.

John and Sean had been planning for weeks to take a couple of teams over. As soon as Cormac heard, he said he'd come along. The teams were Stan, Tom, Lucy, who was back from college, Cathy, an old flame of Sean's, brunette and attractive, Danny and Pickles, the Lanigan twins.

The Lanigan twins were identical and notorious in Coventry. They looked alike and spoke alike, not many could tell them apart. Although almost reformed they both had led a life of thievery and had made excellent use of their doppelganger characteristics, each blaming the other for whatever mischief they had been up to, "It was my bruffer your honour," their regular get out of jail card.

Stan and John were driving, Cormac was in the van with spare stock. As the venture was both work and pleasure, they planned to find a cheap hotel in the central red-light area of Amsterdam.

They left early on Monday, getting to the Ferry for ten, leaving plenty of time to get a late breakfast. The crossing was on the rough side, one or two spending most of the time on deck trying to stave off seasickness. They arrived in Holland, cleared the ferry terminal, and headed north. The weather was damp but within an hour, they'd reached

THE PICTURE GAME

the outskirts of Amsterdam. In the centre of town, they asked around for accommodation and managed to get rooms above a café, spartan but cheap.

In the earlier Fords Transits, a solid thump to the back of the van would open the rear doors, rendering the locks useless. So before settling in Cormac wanted to know where he could park safely. Erik the cafe owner, a ginger hippy Viking type, offered his garage for the van. But the cars would have to take their chances parked on the road or in a public car park. Once that was settled, they went to their rooms. Sean and Cormac shared, the girls were together, Tom was with John, next door to Danny and Pickles.

After a bit of planning for the week, it was out for food, a few beers and of course a look around the red-light district. The evening was colder than expected and after being out for fifteen minutes, they returned to the digs to get coats. After a once around they split up, with Cormac, Sean, John and Tom together. The girls went their own way, leaving Stan with Danny and Pickles to cruise by themselves.

Beautiful girls were advertising their wares behind full-length windows and would wave to the punters as they gawked in. Drugs were for sale, dealers would sidle up whenever they stood still, anything from heroin to weed. An enticing slim blond girl who looked less jaded than the rest caught their eye. She called herself Kitty, she was nineteen and would do all four for sixty gilders. Sean, John and Tom were eager, but Cormac wasn't so interested. After a bit of negotiation, they agreed all four for fifty-five guilders, for an hour. The time was mostly filled with giggles of embarrassment as they waited their turn outside but one after another, they all finished with ten minutes to spare. John who'd been first asked for an extra blowjob but Kitty refused. They promised to come back later in the week, Kitty smiled, she'd heard that before.

As they wandered through the narrow streets, a bare-

165

chested stud, whistled and beckoned them over. "Hey boys, drinks half price," he said in a strong Dutch accent.

Only when they got closer, seeing the posters with half-dressed muscle men, jockstraps and leather caps, did the penny drop.

"Fuck, it's a queers club," John said, mouth agape.

"Come on, let's go in," said Sean, intrigued. "They ain't gonna fuck us."

The stud passed out the free voucher, "I keep a few for you, tell the guys you are friends of mine. Christian, okay!"

The boys were up for it even just for a free drink.

Christian walked them past the unmanned reception and down into the club, which was dingy and cold. He pointed at a barman "Give it to him, my friend Jules," and left.

The music was thumping, disco with a trance-like beat. A few men were on the dancefloor, writhing in dark courtship. The barman took their vouchers and handed over the glasses of beer. Unlike the feminine gays they had expected, most were muscular and heavyset. Some were dressed in leather, others were in work clothes, with shoulders exposed.

Sean was whispering something in John's ear when a man roughly brushed past.

"What the fuck's his game?" said John, clenching his glass. Tom looked over his shoulder, ready to go if needs be.

The man was wearing tight denim jeans, grey t-shirt and baseball cap. He stood with his back against the bar and lit a cigarette, looking out across the dancefloor.

"I don't think he's queer. He probably thought we were," Sean said.

Tom said, "Nah, he's queer alright."

The guy looked casually over, dragged on his smoke, and then turned to face the bar, surly and aggressive.

"Come on, let's get out of here," said John, gulping

THE PICTURE GAME

down his drink. "Fucking queers."

Christian looked disappointed as they passed him in the doorway.

"Not for us mate," called John.

On the way back to the accommodation they bought burger and chips from a kiosk, an Arab guy handing it through a window. Tom bought a bag of weed from a cross eyed dealer, who tried to cheat them but the lads weren't having any of it. It had been a long day, what with the driving, the crossing and the shagging, once in their beds, they were out like lights.

Cormac was early to rise and after a quick wash, went out for a walk. Later the sellers drifted into Erik's café for breakfast, chatting over the previous night.

Lucy had skipped breakfast too and found herself wandering along about twenty yards behind Cormac. Having tried to cop off with him and getting blanked, he wasn't on the top of her most wanted list. So she didn't make any effort to catch up.

At one of the clubs he slowed and looked through the windows. It was obviously a gay club, Bruno's, with butch men plastered on advertising posters. "If he's not gay, I'm the Virgin Mary," she smiled. "That would explain the knockback." she thought to herself.

Positioning herself by the window opposite she could see his reflection trying to appear casually as he looked at the posters. She watched as he moved off. After fifty yards, he stopped at a music shop, then turned back towards the club, as he passed, he slowed once again.

It was after midday when the teams loaded up and headed out on the shift. Cormac now had the rest of the day to himself. He bought a breakfast burger and with the sun was shining, he wandered out into the street. There was only a fraction of tourists, compared to the previous evening. Families with children wandered past half-dressed girls, cannabis cafés and sex boutiques. Cormac pondered on the different attitude back home, where sex

167

THE PICTURE GAME

shops and prostitution were strictly taboo, always behind closed doors and blacked-out window. He crossed back and forth over the canals, past the numerous boats and barges. The tinkle of bicycle bells was constant as students and workers went about their business. Finding an empty bench, he sat to eat. Keen-eyed birds, flocked over as he unwrapped his burger and made himself comfortable. A couple joined him, feeding the pigeons corners off their sandwiches. Cormac watched as the birds scrambled for the scraps. He asked the couple where they were from, they simply smiled unable to communicate.

In Chinatown, a thin blond boy, arms folded across his chest was leaning against a wall, viewing his prospects. Anonymity gave Cormac courage, he waited opposite, the boy gestured with a nod and strolled over. Cormac followed him upstairs into a cubicle with a bed. His name was Filippus. He was nineteen and had dropped out of college to travel but after catching Dengue fever in Chile came home. The sex was Cormac's usual blend of lust and violence. After two minutes, Filippus stopped and made him pay an extra ten guilders, or he would not go on. As he was leaving, Filippus handed him a card.

"This is for you, your kind of place. Try it."

On the card was an image of a sneering muscleman in leather. The name 'Club Blau' was printed in German poster style font.

"It's on the next corner, left side," said Filippus.

Cormac thanked him and slipped the card in his top pocket.

"You around most days?" Cormac asked.

"Most days."

"Yeah, maybe catch up with you later," said Cormac

"I would like that."

Wary of being found out, Cormac threw the card in a bin on his way back to the lodgings. With time to kill, he remembered that he'd brought a book from home, 'The Old Man and the Sea' by Ernest Hemingway. The only novel he had ever finished was 'A Farewell to Arms', so for now Hemingway was his favourite author. He opened a can of beer and started reading but was asleep before long. He awoke to the sound of John coming in. They both went down to remove the stock from the car to the safety of the van, then went out to a sandwich bar.

When John asked what he'd been up to, Cormac said he'd wandered around in the morning to get some fresh air and spent the rest of the day reading. John complained that Lucy had been funny all day, trying to wind him up. Cormac told him not to worry, she was a funny cow but a decent seller.

"Stan wants to head into town later, I think he wants to dip his wick," John laughed.

"Fucking hell, Stan the dirty bastard. You go, I feel fucked. It's been one of those days. You know, when you've done fuck all," Cormac replied.

They bought some beer and sweets on their way back. Cormac got a newspaper, paying over a guilder for The Sun which pissed him off. Sean was back from the shift by the time they got back. His team had done well, selling three Big 'Uns, twenty smalls and forty-eight meds between them.

John, Stan, Lucy and the rest of the sellers disappeared into the night at around ten. Sean had decided to stay behind with his brother. They shared a few beers and watched TV. After finding nothing decent on telly, Sean glanced at the newspaper, while Cormac went back to his book. Trying to make conversation, Cormac asked where they were planning to hit the following day.

Sean looked up, taking a moment, "Oh, we'll just move on."

Cormac looked over the top of his book at his brother and smiled.

25
The King is Dead

Sully's dead," John cried out, as he yanked Cormac from his slumber.

In panic Cormac yelped in fear, "What?"

"Sully's dead," repeated John, he was sitting on the edge of the bed pulling Cormac up by his t-shirt, his eyes bulging, nose to nose.

What?" Cormac repeated.

He's dead, he's dead." John shouted, "Sully's fucking dead!" He let go of Cormac who slumped back.

Cormac rubbed his eyes and glanced at the clock, it was just after midnight. "Who's dead?"

John looked back at him, it was like a switch had tripped in John's body, the energy sucked out of him, "Sully's dead," he said in barely a whisper. His head dropped into his hands.

"What the fuck's going on?" said Sean, now awake.

"Sully's been killed, stabbed," John turned facing Sean.

Both brothers were now sitting bolt upright.

"It was Dave Feeney, Steve Feeney's brother. Sully was battering Steve, when Dave comes out of the kitchen with a sword and stuck it in Sully," John explained.

"That was Steve Feeney that Sully battered at his party, wasn't it?" Sean said, adding, "I didn't know he had a brother."

"Yeah, he's got three, cunts the lot of them," said John.

"Really, is he dead?" Cormac asked.

THE PICTURE GAME

"He is mate, that's it for Sully. Fucking hell, I still can't believe it myself," replied John.

"Where was he?" Cormac asked.

"Over in Radford," said John, Steve was going on at Sally again, when Sully stepped in. Fucking hell, you try and do the right, eh." He shook his head and went on, "Supposedly even after he was stabbed, he was still giving Steve a beating. Leroy managed to get him into a car to take him to hospital, even though he was saying that he didn't need a doctor. He was alright in the waiting room, even had a Turkish Delight, then collapsed."

"Fucking hell, that's what he had when I took him," Sean smiled.

John and Cormac looked at Sean.

"He did, he had a Turkish Delight," Sean shrugged.

There was a knock at the door. John opened it, it was Lucy and Cathy, along with Danny and Pickles. The girls were sobbing whilst the twins were quiet, sombre faced

Cormac stood up in his underwear, "We need to say a prayer."

They huddled together, arms over each other's shoulders. All Cormac could think to do was the rosary. "Our father who art in heaven…" he finished only one verse,' continuing with, "God, look after our friend Stephen O'Sullivan, take him into your heart…" He stuttered a few more words and gently squeezed his brothers quivering shoulder. "Take him into your heart and love him as we too have loved him. Amen."

Lucy was the first to speak, "Phew, that was nice." She wiped a tear with the back of her sleeve and then going from person to person hugged each in turn.

John opened the one remaining can of beer and handed it around for a toast, each took a swig.

Finally, it came back to John, "Fucking hell it's empty," he laughed shaking the can, but still raised it. "To our old friend Sully."

They managed to get some beer from Erik, the owner

of the café downstairs.

Once he heard of the sad story, Erik also dug out a bottle of whiskey, he would not take any money for it, "To toast your friend's passing," he said handing it over.

Back in Cormac and Sean's bedroom they each took slugs, saying a few words before passing the bottle on. They shared their stories, some good, some bad, all embroidered.

Erik let them use his phone Lucy managed to speak to a few friends in Coventry. The funeral was arranged for the following Friday, taking place in Coventry rather than Sully's hometown of Manchester. Cormac said he would book the return ferry for Thursday and would take care of the cost. The hat went around and they managed fifty quid to buy a wreath, which Lucy would organise through a florist back home. Some of the sellers took it harder than others. Tom, Sean and Danny wanted to work, saying that's what Sully would have done, they were probably right, but Cormac made the decision, they would have a day of mourning.

Sean, Cormac, John and most of the others had stayed up all night. When they awoke, the mood was sombre, partly due to Sully's demise but mainly down to the booze. With the help of a hair of the dog they felt better as the day went on and as they headed for the night, they were all in good spirits.

The hard liquor flowed freely as they cruised from bar to bar. They passed the prostitute from the previous night, giggling, Sean nudged his brother.

Stan and Pickles went over to haggle.

"Go on Stan, get in there, there's the door," John called over, pointing to the side entrance.

Stan glanced over and winked.

Lucy veiled her remark saying, "Doesn't Cormac prefer the backdoor?"

It didn't register with anyone apart from Cormac, who shot her an enquiring look.

THE PICTURE GAME

At midnight they found themselves in Molly Malone's, a brick fronted Irish pub which felt familiar to the pubs back home. Stan reappeared, giving the thumbs up, Pickles had decided to head back to the hotel. They were sharing a wooden long table with a group of Brummies. One or two heads were dropping, but most were still going strong. Cormac had intentionally slowed down, keeping his eye on Lucy who had cornered John and was whispering something.

The Brummies started up the Irish rebel songs. Then one thought it funny to slag off Coventry, which didn't go down well with John. He threw a punch, next fists and glasses were flying. John bust his knuckle on a fat Brummie skull but apart from that no-one was seriously injured. On their way back they sang their way through another rendition of Whiskey in the Jar.

Lucy stopped and had everyone huddle together to look up at the stars. She gazed up, "That's him," pointing at the brightest.

By now it was past two o'clock in the morning. The night air was cold and damp and potato fritters their post-midnight feast.

Despite his damaged hand, John was up early organising the stock. Lucy wandered over, bleary-eyed. She was not a natural beauty but was busty, trim and ballsy, with make-up on was a six out of ten, without it, she looked like a man.

"Heavy night," she said, putting her hand to her head.

"Yeah, how are you feeling?" John replied, taking a second look at her.

She didn't answer but let out a lazy whistle.

John chuckled, "Well, that fucker would have approved."

Lucy paused in contemplation, glancing up at the sky. "Yeah, he missed a good one," she smiled as she picked up a pile of pictures of a small wall.

"They need to go back in the van," John said, stacking

THE PICTURE GAME

the prints.

"How's yer man, have you spoke to him?" she called as she carried the pictures across.

John knew what she meant; she wasn't up this early for her health. She was worried about what she had said about Cormac.

John paused to consider her motivation, he knew she'd been knocked back by Cormac and wondered if this was her way of justifying the rejection. But then again, maybe she was telling the truth, Cormac was never a 'ladies' man like his brother, but the hooker? Nah, he wasn't gay. Lucy was trying to wind him up.

"He's good, sleeping off the booze," he said counting the pictures from the boot.

Lucy carried over another pile, placing them alongside. Neither felt comfortable, so in silence they finished loading.

The ferry left just before midnight, and was due in early on Thursday. This gave them plenty of time before the funeral. The roads were clear and the drive home was easy, arriving in Coventry just before daybreak.

Ma was pleased to see them but flabbergasted at the news of Sully's demise. Fearful of trouble, she suggested perhaps it was best that they did not attend the funeral. But on realizing she could not dissuade them, decided to go herself.

The funeral was held at St Anne's and well attended by the picture selling community, sombre and smartly turned out in black. Sue was with Stan who looked the odd man out, dressed in a brown bomber jacket over jeans.

A tall, elegant woman, grey hair pulled back in an Alice band was at the front and was later introduced as Sarah, Sully's mother. Alongside her stood a thin dark-haired girl, Jilly, Sully's sister, of perhaps twelve or thirteen who cried continuously throughout the service. Sully's father was not present, no one thought it appropriate to ask why.

THE PICTURE GAME

The service was short and simple without the formality of a mass. A good few went up to eulogize, the usual tearjerkers, even Fucked up Freddie got up sharing his spittle with the congregation. The family followed the coffin as it was led out and stood at the back to receive condolences.

Sean spotted Veronica, she was dressed in black, her look of cool sophistication stood out from the rest of the crowd. He was unsure if he should approach, but at the graveside, she slipped in beside him.

"Hello stranger," she whispered.

He simply smiled.

The priest was droning earnestly, the funeral-goers were getting impatient, shuffling from side to side, some whispering, the odd laugh rising above the drone. A bitter wind was blowing, with ladies holding onto their hats. Of the mourners who had arrived from Manchester, it was fair to say they were not your average social surfer types. A mix of bull-necked scar-faced men and thick-set overly made-up women, with a smattering of hatchet faces of either sex. They made the Coventry crowd look positively genteel. A particularly menacing-looking thug was asking for information on the Feeney brothers.

Just as the service finished, the heavens opened. Sean put his arm around Veronica's waist as they dashed towards the car park. Cormac and Ma were waiting there.

"I'm so sorry to hear about your boyfriend. I didn't know him well, but he seemed such a lovely man," said Ma.

She warmly hugged Veronica, whose response was muted.

The wake was held at The Chase Hotel, a mock Tudor building on the London Road. The receptionist led them through to a large corporate-looking room, oak panelled, a chandelier in the middle. Not everyone at the funeral had made it, but the room was full. Tea and biscuits were free, but if you wanted a pint you had to pay. Ladies arrived in

175

THE PICTURE GAME

aprons carrying through platters of sandwiches.

Cormac and Ma waited in turn to say a few words to Sully's mother. Sarah introduced one of the bull-necked men, as Sully's Uncle Mick. Despite his menacing appearance, he was the epitome of a gentleman, kind and polite. However, he did have a peculiar habit, in that he would cover his mouth as he talked.

Sean and Veronica had sat themselves at a table. He told her of the developments in the business, of him and John now owning their own teams. Veronica smiled and raised her glass in celebration. He went on telling her about their trip to Amsterdam, leaving out the hooker. She said she was now only modelling part-time and had a job managing a boutique. Neither mentioned why she had not been in touch.

The afternoon clocked on to evening, some guests left and a few more arrived.

Sully's mother sat smiling sphinx like, she had packed away her tears and placed them somewhere else for later. Uncle Mick had just bought a round of whiskies for the men, sherry for the ladies, watching as they were handed out. He tapped on his glass and the room went silent. He made a short speech thanking everyone for attending, once again sharing some embroidered stories before going on.

"Stephen," he raised his hand to his mouth, then consciously put it down. "Sully, my nephew is now in heaven. You all knew him and I'm sure like me, loved him. Please raise your glass to the memory of Stephen O'Sullivan."

Everyone stood and toasted his memory.

There was a bit of a tussle as Uncle Mick shared a few words with one of the more menacing mourners. The bruiser leant aggressively forward, his hands on the table.

"God has the power to forgive," he gazed around the room, eyes slowly going from group to group. His voice lowered to a menacing growl, "That's God's gift," once more his eyes cruised the room. "His gift alone."

176

THE PICTURE GAME

Cormac felt the hairs on the back of his neck rise. There were whispers as to what he meant. To Cormac it was clear that the Finney's had better hope the jury find them guilty.

Through the crowd, a familiar figure appeared. It was Billy. Like Veronica, he stood out, looking like an eccentric diplomat on a state visit. Cormac smiled watching as he shook hands with the people he passed.

He embraced Sully's mum, they held on to each other, she smiled warmly and pulled him closer. On seeing Billy, Uncle Micks sombre face changed into a beaming smile, he looked Billy up and down, as they shared a joke, they too embraced. By their body language they were familiar friends.

Picking up his beer, Cormac walked over to where Sean and Veronica were sitting. "Look what the cat's dragged in," he said with a wink, as he pulled out a chair.

Billy glanced up and waved across. Uncle Mick too, he then leant forward into Billy ear, cover his mouth and whispered something.

"Hello gorgeous," said Billy, as he approached and kissed Veronica's cheek.

He shook hands with the boys. They shuffled out a chair for him.

"First things first," he said. "Can I get anyone a drink? I've been on that motorway for two and a half hours and I am parched."

Cormac jumped up apologetically and took the drinks order. He asked Billy if he thought Sully's mum and uncle might like one but Billy told him not to bother. He explained that he'd a very important business deal to finalise in the morning, and unfortunately had not been able to get to the funeral.

He exuded charm as he lit one of his black cigarettes, the smell was strong and exotic. Sean asked what was in them? Billy explained that they were flavoured with cloves and cinnamon and that he had them sent over from

177

THE PICTURE GAME

Indonesia. Cormac returned with the drinks as Ma wandered over to say she was heading home and getting a lift from John. Billy stood up, remarking how proud she must be of such wonderful sons, and was amazed that she was old enough to have had them.

Ma had seen his type before, but as her grandmother would say, "Mr Flattery was always welcome."

Once Ma had gone, they talked of Sully, of what a shock it was. Billy asked what they knew about the Feeney family. All they could tell him was that they were from Willenhall, a particularly rough part of the city. They were a big family, maybe eight or nine, who regularly drank in The Bear, a harpy of a mother and a useless wastrel drunk of a father. They were the dregs of their community. The boys had all done a stretch, the girls were usually pregnant at fifteen, looking like old bags by the time they were twenty-five. Scrap cars sat in their front yard and dog shit everywhere. Billy shook his head. They didn't have an address but if they were to ask on the estate, anyone would know them. Billy asked how business was going. He was pleased to hear that Cormac had re-focused his time, leaving Sean and John to manage the selling side.

It was now seven thirty and once again the ladies in aprons arrived with sandwiches accompanied by chicken drumsticks, pork pies and salad. Cormac and Sean joined the queue, leaving Billy and Veronica alone. Whilst waiting in line Sean watched the two of them, it was obvious that they were more familiar with each other than he had expected.

As they chatted, Billy leant in and kissed Veronica a peck on the lips.

Cormac nudged his arm, "Did you see that?"

"Yeah." It hit him like a red-hot bolt, his anger ignited.

Despite promising to bring over food for Veronica, he only picked up a single plate. They made their way back, Billy jumped up from Sean's seat and went back to his original chair. Stubbornly Sean insisted Billy sit next to

178

THE PICTURE GAME

Veronica, Billy refused laughing him off.

Veronica looked at the single plate.

"Do you fancy some food?" she asked Billy.

Billy went to get up.

"No don't worry I'll get it for you," as she looked down at Sean. If her sneer could be scored, this was about an eight out of ten.

Sean sat cold and silent and after a few minutes of sulking, wandered off to talk to Lucy. A half-hour later Cormac too wandered off to where Sean and Lucy were. They were joined by a timid looking Sue, she'd been watching from the wings as the scene played out, perhaps all was not lost. Sean was in a belligerent mood, knocking down pint after pint. He returned to the buffet table with Sue by his side, hoping to provoke some sort of reaction. Veronica, didn't even look up, her cool elegance apparent. However, a smouldering Stan was watching, anger brewing. When enough eyes were on him, Sean not so subtly led Sue into the men's toilets, returning a few minutes later grinning. Stan flew at him in a jealous rage, but was stopped from doing any serious damage by Cormac. Sean sneered, it was obvious that he was simply using Sue. After Cormac pulled Stan off Sean a second time, he suggested that they leave, Sean agreed, leaving Sue to face the music.

A bemused Billy walked them out into the car park, he wanted a word with Cormac. Sean watched, his emotions simmering, as Billy chatted to his brother. He took a few steps closer, trying to earwig in on their conversation.

Billy was saying he was having another party, this time at Christmas. He would be sending out the invites if they wanted to come. Before returning he turned to Sean. "Perhaps you should be more careful, one day life may trip you up," it was offered as sincere advice, rather than a veiled threat.

On the drive home, Cormac laughed at his brother's boldness, "You're some man," he flashed a smile.

179

Sean grinned, unsure of his hollow victory.

As they hit the London Road, 'Brown Sugar', came on the radio, Cormac blasted up the volume. "I fucking love the Stones," as he bashed out the beat on the steering wheel. "Remember Sully's party?"

Sean smiled wistfully.

Cormac glanced across at his brother, "Like the man said, Fuck her!"

26
The Trouble with Ma

As autumn inched into winter, things settled into a rhythm with Cormac and Sean keeping out of each other's way. If there was friction, John would act as a go-between, calming them both.

Although the whispers got louder regarding his sexuality, Cormac ignored them, even going as far as renting a small flat to take his lovers to. The occasional bogus business event allowed him nights away. His predilection for rough trade was showing no signs of abating, now often involving several partners.

Whilst Cormac had recently discovered the carnal pleasures of the flesh, Sean was years ahead. The fall out with Veronica seemed to have filled his sails, and his extra cash didn't go unnoticed.

But as Sean and Cormac enjoyed their flings their mother was lacking the nourishment they once provided. It was now the third time she had been to see Dr Davis. On each visit he patiently listened as she dragged her empty soul onto his patient's chair.

As far as Cormac and Sean were concerned, dinner was always ready, beds made, toilets cleaned, and washing done.

One Tuesday evening when Cormac returned home, Ma was not in the house. He checked every room. It was in the icy cold garden that he found her sitting in her nightie.

THE PICTURE GAME

"Is that you Timmy?" Ma's ghostlike eyes stared.

"No, it's me Ma, what are you doing outside?" Taking her by the arm, he led her indoors setting her down on her chair. He lit the fire and put an overcoat over her shoulders.

She seemed agitated, unsure of where she was.

"Timmy, you've been away all day, I got worried and went to look for you," Ma looked up.

Cormac was sitting on the arm of the chair, stroking her hair. Slowly, she began to settle. He made a cup of tea and rang his Auntie Aggie for advice. Fifteen minutes later Aggie knocked on the door.

After chatting with Cormac, she went through to see her sister. Aggie was her elder sister by two years, Ma was used to being bossed about by her.

"Now what's come over you Mary, freezing yourself to death in the middle of winter?" Aggie spoke gently, as though talking to a child.

Ma didn't speak, instead she raised a finger to her lips, "Shush, the boys are asleep."

Aggie looked over to Cormac

"Mary, it's me, Aggie. Are you okay?"

This time her voice was sharper, more like a firm teacher. Ma smiled at her from a different world. A world where her boys were little, both sitting on her knee, shuffling and barging to get closer. She raised her arms, cuddling the spirits of their childhood.

Her voice fragmented, "Where are they Timmy? Where are the boys?"

Cormac knelt beside her holding her delicate fingers, "I'm here mummy." He placed her hand on his head, she gently stroked him.

"Where are they Timmy?" her shoulders heaved and from the depth of her soul rose up a long and mournful moan.

Aggie phoned the doctor's surgery, as it was late it automatically went through to a girl on the switchboard

THE PICTURE GAME

who said they would send an emergency doctor over.

About an hour later, the doctor arrived, he introduced himself as Dr Patel. As he approached Ma, she looked startled and pulled the overcoat around her. It took a while for Aggie and Cormac to persuade her that Dr Davis could not attend, this was Dr Patel.

Dr Patel was probably in his early thirties. He had a lively eye, a dark beard and wore a turban. He stood patiently until Ma agreed for him to attend, but only if Timmy, her husband, was by her side. Cormac sat on the edge of her chair.

After chatting for a while, he began asking questions. "Did she know where she was? What day was it? Who was here in the room?"

He took her pulse, listened to her heart and took her temperature. He sat facing her, calmly, head over to one side.

He asked Aggie about Ma's early life. Had she had any incidents like this before, or had any other member of her family suffered anything similar?

Aggie relayed the history of the Kelly family, of saints and sinners, she paused, and asked Cormac if he could leave the room. Ma watched as he left.

"Timmy are you off to work?" she asked.

I'll be back soon," said Cormac.

Aggie watched as Cormac closed the door to the living room. Aggie took the doctor to the corner of the room and in a whisper, she went on. Mary had been by far the prettiest of the sisters. They had lived in a two-bedroom cottage, ten of them, including their parents. They grew up in a small rural community where everyone knew everyone. Their father was a musician, mostly the accordion but could turn his hand to any instrument. Mary loved Irish dancing and had reached the all-Ireland finals, two years running. Mary and her father would put on shows at the local pub, and sometimes further afield, the crowd loved them.

THE PICTURE GAME

Dr Patel stopped her and raised his hand, "Can you tell me if Mrs Finn has suffered from any mental illness, please?"

Aggie coolly looked him up and down, "If you could let me finish doctor."

She continued, when Mary was twelve or thirteen their mother had an excessive bleed giving birth to her ninth child, both she and the baby had died. Her death affected the whole family, their father the worst. Gone was the happy man, treating himself to a couple of pints of Guinness at the weekend, and in his place arrived a cold and sadistic man drinking whisky day and night straight from the bottle. Mary, and her father had a closeness that he didn't share with the rest of his children, she'd always been his favourite. One night in a drunken stupor, he took her to his bed. He said she was to keep him warm, but Mary cried for weeks. Not a word was said outside the family, nor inside for that matter.

Dr Patel nodded slowly.

"I'm not finished yet doctor," said Aggie.

It was the night of the second anniversary of their mother's death that he went on another bender. When there was still no sign of him two days later, they went out to look for him. It was Mary who found him dead in a ditch. It was thought he'd had a massive stroke but that was never diagnosed. Mary left for Liverpool before he was buried. Two weeks after arriving she was sectioned for four weeks in a mental institution and never returned to Ireland.

Dr Patel shook his head and looked at Ma, she looked back with pleading eyes.

When Cormac returned, the doctor was packing up his things. In her hands, Aggie had a small strip of pills along with a prescription. As the doctor was leaving, he said Ma would need a lot of rest, and they should contact the local doctor in the morning if things got worse. Cormac shook his hand and thanked him as he closed the door.

184

THE PICTURE GAME

It was late on Thursday when Sean showed up. Despite his own carousing Cormac took him to task. "Where have you been? You never think of the family," said Cormac, as he followed him to the kitchen.

Sean looked tired but was chirpy, only offering a sideways smirk as he popped the kettle on. Cormac continued to berate him, Sean turned angrily to face his brother. At that moment, Ma appeared in the doorway.

"Sean, Sean, My darling boy is home."

Sean responded with a soft, "Hey."

He held her in a warm embrace. It was as though a cloud were lifted. Ma was beaming as Sean walked his mother back to her chair. A few seconds later Cormac arrived with the teas, a face like thunder.

"Can I speak to Sean for a little while Ma? I need to tell him something," asked Cormac.

Sean looked up.

"Just for a minute," Cormac's tone was calm and authoritative.

"I'll have a quick chat with Cormac and I'll be back."

Cormac explained the change in Ma's behaviour, "She's not well, she doesn't know where she is, half the time she thinks she a kid back in Ireland, thinks I'm granddad, or dad. She tried to kiss me, for fuck's sake."

Sean laughed, Cormac smiled too shaking his head.

"What are we going to do?" Sean asked.

Cormac said that Aunt Aggie was coming over in the daytime, but the mornings and evenings was down to them.

"I can't do evening, I'm out on the shift," said Sean defensively.

Cormac had already worked it out, saying that he'd take care of the evenings, but it was for Sean to look after her in the morning. The weekends they would take it in turns.

Sean glanced up hesitantly, before asking, "Did the doctor say anything about her going into a home?"

THE PICTURE GAME

"You're some cunt, you are," replied Cormac, walking back into the front room.

Despite their plans, Ma became more and more confused, her behaviour was unpredictable and impulsive. It was on finding her on the kitchen floor with the coalman, that Aggie made the call to have her sectioned. The neighbours were all out asking questions as Aggie helped Ma into the ambulance. She was placed into the psychiatric ward at the Walsgrave Hospital, where she would not be allowed to leave and her medication would be controlled.

The six weeks she spent there went by quickly. For the first two weeks Ma was unsure whether she was awake or was dreaming. In her dreams, she fell in love with an Asian man, who was kind to her on her first day, although she hadn't seen him since.

As Aggie worked on the maternity ward of the hospital, she called in every day to visit, the boys once or twice a week. It wasn't until the fourth week that Aggie thought she could see a change, Ma seemed to be returning to her old self.

Eventually, the doctors discharged Ma into Aggie's care, who'd agreed to let her stay with her for a few weeks.

"Until your Ma is back on her feet," Aggie suggested to the boys.

Despite the guilt, the boys had no objections. The routine of Aggie coming home from work, them sharing meals and evening together seemed to have a stabilising effect. If not quite on the crest of a wave, Ma was far from the depths of despair she suffered only a couple of months ago.

Although she never mentioned it, Ma had enjoyed her dance with madness, during that time the world had become a magical place where the gods had shared some of their secrets. But once she'd moved back home, reality again descended. Within a couple of days, the boys went

186

THE PICTURE GAME

back to their usual routines. And despite her medication, the edginess was never far away. Aggie visited every day to check on her. Ma was beginning to resent her sister's intrusion, and when she flew at Aggie with a knife, Aggie gave up, with Ma having to return to the hospital for another few weeks.

27
A second Invitation

It was during the first week of December the invitation arrived, this time decorated with Zeus, who had transformed into a swan as he ravished Leda. It was a New Year's Eve party; Billy had presumably thought it a better date.

On seeing the image, Sean pondered its significance, Cormac had already looked it up in his book of Greek myths, leaving Sean in their bedroom reading the story.

Ma liked the image, and once the picture was framed, she displayed it prominently on her mantlepiece, despite Aggie's disapproval. A change had come over Ma, she had dyed her hair a rich auburn, she had lost a lot of weight, her figure and jawline had returned. She looked ten years younger, maybe more.

John remarked to Sean that his brother Paddy had asked Ma out.

Sean didn't believe him but asked her about it.

Ma laughed it off, "Are you daft? What would young Paddy be doing with an old woman like me."

The explanation seemed to satisfy Sean.

The date of the party crept closer, again, they rented their tuxedos. The assistant in the men's department, as camp as a Christmas tree fairy, was a very recent friend of Cormac's. And with 'his' very generous discount they opted for the designer range. This included a quality wool suit fabric, cufflinks, a silk pocket square, along with cummerbunds. It was a step up for them both.

In the meantime, Ma was making plans for her own New Year's Eve party. Christ The King club was putting on a do, and a little bird had mentioned that Paddy Kelly might be there. With a lot of persuading and cajoling, Aggie, who had not been out since October 1967, agreed to go along. Christ the King was in Coundon, the Irish heartland of Coventry, nicknamed County Coundon. It was a few miles away from Ma's closer option, The Finbarr's, but she was wise enough not to play too close to home. As she waved her sons off, she didn't watch them disappear up the road as usual, but quickly closed the door to get herself ready.

28
Billy's Party Part II

They turned into Plymouth Street, and parked outside Denmark House, in the same spot as Sully had before.

"Bloody hell, it doesn't seem like a year does it?" said Cormac.

Sean shook his head laughing. "It's not a year, it's only six months."

Cormac's brain clicked around a notch as he laughed. "Bloody hell, you're right."

"Daft fuck," said Sean, jeering his brother.

A fresh-faced red-haired pageboy boy greeted them. He used a small gavel, giving the door a couple of solid bangs and with a creak the door opened. Inside the heat pressed against them with every step they took. It was more formal than the summer party. The music was old and respectable, with a jazz quartet playing to a polite audience in the corner. Ladies of all ages were wandering around in evening gowns, some sleeveless, some backless, others in what could be described as frontless. The men were dressed in black dinner suits, some in full tails, more penguin-like than the rest. The loose shenanigans from the summer party had gone and, in its place, a middleclass formality.

They spotted Hugo, as he entertained a group of thin ladies, jewels jangling in laughter at his wit, even he appeared toned down from their previous visit.

A young waitress silently appeared with a tray of

THE PICTURE GAME

drinks. They helped themselves to a couple of champagne flutes and ventured in deeper.

29
Picking up Aggie

The taxi was booked for a return with Flannigan's and arrived at Ma's for seven. It was only a five minutes journey to pick up Aggie. The driver was Mick O'Toole. Mick asked what was taking her out as far as Christ the King. Ma answer, telling him that the last couple of years the Finbarr's was so ram-packed, you couldn't get a drink, or a seat, you couldn't even hear the band with the row. Mick sympathised but warned her not to expect too much difference at Christ the King.

Ma shrugged, "Well, a change is as good as a rest, isn't that so Mick?"

Mick agreed. They pulled up outside Aggie's, he parped the horn. They sat for a few moments staring at Aggie's front door. With a huff, Ma got out, and gave it a solid bang, and dashed back to the car, it was freezing. Again, with eyes affixed, they sat waiting for her sister to appear.

"She'll be applying a few finishing touches, no doubt," said Mick, as he rubbed his whiskers.

Ma was halfway out of the car, when Aggie appeared wrapped in a long fur coat and hat.

"Jaysus, it's the Tsarina herself," Mick laughed.

Ma couldn't help but chuckle as she held the door open for her sister.

The two sisters got out at the club and wanting to confirm his return, Ma said, "Will I pay you now Mick?"

THE PICTURE GAME

Mick knew score, "No, you can pay me later Mary."

"What time will you be back?"

"One o'clock on the dot," Mick called out, as he pulled away.

Ma produced two tickets to the wiry septuagenarian sitting in the booth, half a Guinness lodged in front of him. Without a word he ripped a corner and handed them back.

They checked in their coats and hats, Aggie mentioning to the young attendant to take good care of her furs. Underneath her coat Ma was wearing a jade brocade dress which stopped at her knee, she looked beautiful, a picture of elegance. A few of the men turned their heads to get a glimpse, only to receive a jab in the ribs from their jealous wives. Aggie didn't match her sister in the attention stakes but scrubbed up well in her maroon wool skirt and black lambswool sweater.

At the bar, they ordered Southern Comforts and lemonade and found themselves a table. Looking around they nodded at a few acquaintances and sipped on their drinks.

30
Special Bullshit

"Hello," said the Brigadier smiling, "It's good to see you again. I do hope you found your brother, you were looking for last time we met."

His grey whiskers were standing straight up and to attention. It was the old boy and his wife from the summer party. His wife held up her lorgnette, inspecting the young men in front of her.

The brigadier looked to his wife before going on, "Don't you remember? This is the young man asking for help to find his brother, in the summer." He repeated louder, "In the summer, dear."

She paused, "Is this the young man who was brawling with some other," her brain skipping this way and that, before spluttering out, "…Youth?"

"What! What did you say?" replied the Brigadier, bending an ear.

"I think you must be mistaking me for someone else," said Cormac

"What! What did you say?" repeated the Brigadier, as the boys wandered off.

They went from room to room, they were looking out for either Billy, Veronica or Francis. A younger group, aged from eighteen to twenty-five, were clustered around a middle-aged grey-haired man, indoor sunglasses perched on his head. He seemed to have his audience captivated. Cormac and Sean wandered over to eavesdrop. A young

THE PICTURE GAME

woman in the group called out to them. It was Rose, Sully's ex-wife, who introduced them.

The older man halted his story, smiling, waiting to continue. Once he had everyone's attention again, he went on. "Yes, a decent bunch of lads, when I first picked them up, they couldn't hold a tune, but they didn't take too long. But you know how these things are, as soon as they released 'Gangsters,' and hit the big time, they sacked me, I should have made millions."

"Ah right, you knew The Specials?" Sean asked.

"Before they were famous," the grey-haired man replied defensively.

Cormac cut in saying, "We knew Terry Hall, he lived up by the football ground." Heads turned looking at Cormac. "Yeah, he's a decent guy, quiet though. You wouldn't think he'd be lead singer in The Specials."

This connection raised their stock with the Two-Tone hungry group. The grey-haired man looked flustered, particularly when Cormac asked him questions which he fussed and faffed to answer. Exiting when the going was good, the so-called 'manager' wandered off, no doubt with another tall tale.

31
Christ The King

Agnes pointed to a particularly young, healthy-looking couple. The man had a crew cut, his wife was blonde and statuesque, head and shoulders above the crowd, it was her neighbours, the Kulczyks.

On catching their eye, Aggie waved over, "They're Ukrainians. A lovely couple," she whispered in her sister's ear. "He works at the Morris, she's a hairdresser."

Ma smiled and courteously waved across.

"What a beautiful couple," Agnes's eyes followed them as they made their way to the bar.

Ma couldn't give a monkey's about the Ukrainians or the Russians for that matter. Her eyes flicked to the door for one reason only, Paddy Kelly.

"Would you like another drink?" she asked her sister, raising herself from the chair.

Aggie looked at her half full glass and then to Ma's empty one, "I will, but make it a bitter lemon this time," she replied.

Ma grabbed her handbag and she made her way to the bar. The club had a system when it was busy. Customers queued at one end and worked their way along the bar until served. Ma took her place, as she waited, she reached into her purse, fiver at the ready.

Behind her was a midget-sized man who was standing with his pint of Guinness only half drunk.

"Best not to let her run dry," he remarked with a

twinkling eye.

Ma ordered a bitter lemon for Aggie, and a double Southern Comfort and lemonade for herself. After bringing the drinks back to their table, she nipped off to the ladies to reapply her make-up.

A pretty young girl of no more than seventeen was doing the same. The young girl smiled with a youthful allure.

Ma looked yearningly at her, "Just a kitten, with life still waiting for you," Ma thought, as she watched the young girl paint her cupid lips.

Looking back at herself from the mirror Ma could see the signs of aging, faint wrinkles on her forehead, laughter lines surrounding her eyes, her lips not as full as they used to be. "Had youth escaped her as she was doing up her apron strings?" Puckering up she flicked her lipstick from side to side. A quick check in the mirror and she left.

The showband played some well-known Irish tunes, reels and jigs, mixed in with a sprinkling from the 'Hit Parade.' The Emerald Five, with a subtitle of The McGarry Family, were dressed in matching white spangled outfits. Mrs McGarry was out front and the singer. She introduced the rest of the band.

"Now I love him to bits," she let go a crafty wink at the audience; a few laughs went up. "My long-suffering husband Peter, on the accordion and trumpet."

Peter, let off a few notes from the accordion.

A cheer, went up.

"We've got Liam and Eugene, my gorgeous sons on guitar."

They let fly a blast of rhythm and bass guitar.

Another cheer.

"And last of all, my beautiful daughter Carol, on backing vocals and drums."

Carol peeled off a drum roll, to cheers and a few wolf whistles.

Mrs McGarry smiled and applauded her family, then

turned to face the audience. "Now's here's one I'm sure you'll all know. It's a great tune to get up and dance to, so let's have a few more on the dancefloor."

Up struck the opening bars, the ska beat unmistakable.

"*My Boy Lollipop...*"

"Come on, let's get up to this one, I love it," said Ma imploring her sister, who was out of her seat already.

Handbags in front of them and smiles from Mrs McGarry they bopped, dipped and shook, along with the others bustling to get their space. A middle-aged man with a greasy forehead, dancing like a marionette puppet which had lost a few strings, jerked his way towards them. Ma and Aggie giggled as they edged away from the flailing arms and legs.

32
Cormac wants a Beer

Cormac took Rose to one side, "How are you? I missed you at the funeral," as he offered his condolences.

Rose smiled and hugged Cormac. "I'll miss him. But I'm not that surprised he's gone, he was always a wild one," she said forcing a smile.

"Yeah a handful." Cormac replied.

Her tears had begun to flow.

"Come here," he pulled her back into his embrace.

Rose wiped away her tears and went on to explain why she wasn't at the funeral. She had never got on with Sully's family. They were a bunch of crooks and gangsters, even Sully himself didn't bother with them. But she'd visited his grave to lay a wreath the day after. She mentioned that there was another person there, an older suntanned man called Paul who was leaving flowers. He said he lived Spain and was an old friend of Sully's. He looked like a retired builder.

Cormac said he thought it was most likely Lucas, the guy who started off the picture game, which both surprised, and pleased him.

Sean joined them, he too offered his condolences but soon wandered back to the Hooray Henry and Henrietta's, a tall redhead called Abie, had particularly caught his eye.

A waiter walked by, Cormac picked a couple of glasses off the tray, handing one to Rose as they re-joined the group. Sean was in full flight, dipping deep into his verbal tin of paint, splashing out stories of the duckers and divers he was acquainted with. The Hooray Henry's and Henrietta's loved it, lapping up all that was thrown at them.

Cormac wondered about his brother, and how he changed from a shrinking violet, to the life and soul of the party at the flick of a switch. Cormac had heard all Sean's stories before so making an excuse of going to the loo, he wandered off. The event was like a 1950s Hollywood movie. Big Peter looked like the battered faced bruiser in The Quiet Man, there was also a Spencer Tracy, a couple of Marilyn Monroes, and a mysterious Greta Garbo. He spotted Billy along with Veronica, both looking fantastic. Billy had cut his hair and now looked like Charlie Watts from the Rolling Stones. Veronica looked like herself but with her hair pulled back, it was Veronica with a hint of Bianca Jagger. They were talking to a potbellied couple, the lady in an outfit resembling a 1920s flapper while the man resembled, Rich Uncle Pennybags, the Monopoly character.

Billy caught his eye and winked and made his excuses to the potbelly duo. It was the usual handshake from Billy and a double air kiss from Veronica.

"I'm glad you made it," he said.

"Did you come on your own?"

"No, me and Sean," replied Cormac.

Billy glanced over Cormac's shoulder, expecting to see Sean in his shadow, then scanned further back into the room.

Veronica's face was cool, betraying nothing.

They spoke about Sully's death while Veronica listened in. A waitress approached carrying a tray of champagne, Veronica took a glass.

Billy picked up two more, but noticing a reluctance from Cormac said, "Oh, would you prefer a beer?"

"I'd love a one," responded Cormac, eyebrows raised merrily.

THE PICTURE GAME

Veronica smiled.

"Listen, we're just gonna get ourselves a couple of beers," said Billy, "We won't be long, will you be okay?"

"Yeah, yeah, I'll be fine," said Veronica and looking up spotted one of the Marilyns waving over.

Cormac followed Billy through the crowd, sharing the odd bit of banter as they went. They pushed through a two-way door to enter the kitchen. There was a din of clattering plates and clinking glasses. Loud rock music was playing but was turned down when Billy entered. Two staff hopped up making themselves busy, one filling wine glasses, the other picked up a tray of canapés and disappeared though the kitchen door heading out into the party.

Billy opened a couple of bottles of German beer, handing one over to Cormac, looked around and barked out a few orders. A middle-aged lady who seemed to be in charge repeated the orders to the minions. He stood for a while overseeing, peering from staff member to staff member.

Billy lowered his voice, "You've gotta watch them. See them two on their arses when we came in?" he raised his eyes. "Probably getting paid fuck all, but the agency is charging me ten quid an hour for the bastards."

"Yeah, I know what you mean," replied Cormac.

As they chatted about Sully and his family. Cormac asked about him and Veronica. "Are you and Veronica an item now?"

Billy smiled, almost laughing, "Veronica and me? No, we're just good friends, she helps me out." He picked up a tray of canapes and offered one to Cormac.

"Is she working for you." Cormac asked as he munched on the small delicacy. "What is that?"

"Beluga caviar, the finest money can buy. Do you like it?

Cormac laughed, "Sully warned us about your food, 'Fishy shit,' he said."

201

THE PICTURE GAME

"Cheeky bastard," Billy laughed. "Yeah, she's running a small boutique for me, I opened it in the summer."

"She's not on the game anymore?" Cormac responded.

Billy looked shocked and surprised, "She's never been on the game, who said she was?

"Maybe I've got the wrong end of the stick, but Sully said she was," Cormac said, backtracking.

Billy laughed, "He was a good lad, but fucking hell he did talk though his arse a lot of the time. Veronica on the game? She's never been on the game!"

Billy's response took Cormac by surprise, he was right about Sully though, he was a bit of a Benny bullshitter.

"Where's Francis these days?" he asked, clutching for a topic to continue the conversation.

Billy picked at the label on his beer bottle, a few seconds went by before he looked up with a faint smile. "Francis? he paused, and swallowed, "Francis is ill." He looked off into the distance. "He's very ill."

"What's the matter with him?" asked Cormac, relieved to be off the subject of Veronica being on the game.

Billy eyes lingered in the distance, he looked confused and fearful, he was about to say something, then changed his mind. He looked to the floor, "We don't know."

THE PICTURE GAME

33
The Siege of Ennis

Looking at the lipstick mark on her glass, Ma decided another trip to the bathroom was necessary. Aggie joined her this time, asking the couple on the next table to watch over their drinks. There was no queue, so whilst Aggie used the facilities, Ma reapplied her lipstick.

"What's up with you Mrs?" said Aggie, washing her hands. "You've had ants in your pants all evening.

Ma looked across at her sister in the mirror, her eyes flashed bright.

"Come out with it, what's going on? I know there's something. Out with it!" Aggie looked indignant, at having not shared her sisters secret.

Ma turned to her sister, the glint had now spread into a full grin. Aggie waited as Ma looked this way and that to check the coast was clear. A rumble of a flushing toilet held them fast with both returning to the sinks. A small bespectacled bird-like woman appeared and without bothering to wash her hands, disappeared.

"Do you know young John who works with the boys?" Ma said with a whisper.

Aggie's eyes narrowed; her bottom lip went out, "I don't really know those fellas, which one is he?"

Ma went on to describe John, his height, his eyes, before giving up on at Aggie's confused expression. She raised her voice, the fringes of her temper beginning to show, "Ah it doesn't matter if you know him or not, it's

203

THE PICTURE GAME

his brother Paddy whose asked me out.

"Fucking hell," Aggie thought to herself, "This one's barely out of the hospital and she's got herself a fancy man." With soft eyes she looked at Ma. "Do you think Mary that's a good idea?"

Ma's brow knitted, her newly painted lips curled with disdain. Picking up her handbag she brushed past her sister, heading back into the club. Aggie didn't follow but stood for a while wondering if she had said the right thing and decided she had.

Ma was at the back of the queue for the bar and was chatting merrily to a weather-beaten navvy of about fifty. Aggie sat down and took a fiver from her purse ready to pay for the drinks. The Emerald Five were finishing off a rendition of Dolly Parton's *Joleen*.

Ma sat down with a thump, splashing Aggie's bitter lemon. They sat in silence, smiling blankly in the direction of the band.

Ma turned, "Did you tell the boys about daddy?" her eyes bored into Aggie.

"Tell them what," Aggie indignantly replied. She knew what her sister meant.

Ma crossed her arms and was about to say something when the navvy leant over her shoulder, smiling. He nodded to Aggie and asked Ma for a dance. Taking a sip of her drink Ma was on her feet, leading the navvy onto the dancefloor.

Aggie watched the pair, the navvy had Ma by the hand, "He's not such a bad dancer, I could go for him myself," Aggie thought. Thinking back to their daddy, Aggie shook her head and gulped back a tear, it was life back then.

The band struck up an Irish reel, *The Siege of Ennis*, where the dancers line up, boy, girl, boy, girl facing one another. The steps are delicate and planned out with a change of partners as they skip back and forth. Ma was an expert and pushed the navvy into place. On a note they were off, it wasn't hard to see who knew the dance, as

THE PICTURE GAME

some seamlessly worked their way up and down the line, whilst others were pushed and pulled across the dancefloor. Ma was, without doubt, the most accomplished. When the dance was over, a crowd gathered around her, with Mrs McGarry applauded her from the stage.

Aggie smiled and felt proud, happy seeing her sister admired.

34
Maybe

With a tap on the shoulder, Sean looked around. It was Veronica, she smiled, greeting him as she did at the graveside. His heart skipped a beat.

"Hello stranger."

Abie, the redhead who Sean was talking to looked up.

"Oh, Hi Veronica, how are you?" in a rich velvety accent.

"Lovely to see you, Abie," said Veronica

They followed the double kiss ritual and then stood back to admire one another.

"You look wonderful," Veronica's voice was different, polished, her manners more refined. "Is Jilly with you?"

Sean watched as they gossiped for a minute or two before Veronica brought him into the conversation.

"I see you've met my husband," Veronica linked her arm through Sean's.

Abie looked confused. Sean smiled beguilingly, happily caught up by Veronica's tale.

"Yes, in the summer we were married under a sacred oak tree at the bottom of the garden," Veronica said elusively.

Sean's mind raced back to the heat of the summer. Now with her body so close, her touch, her scent, he could feel the beginnings of a twitch. He put one hand in his pocket to discreetly adjust himself.

"Oh, you're having me on," laughed Abie.

THE PICTURE GAME

Veronica did not respond but simply lifted an eyebrow.

Abie smirked.

"No, I'm not having you on, and I'm going to steal him away from you this moment." Veronica caught hold of Sean's arm. "Follow me, my love."

Sean looked over his shoulder, grinning at Abie as he was led away. They found a quiet corner, only to be spotted by Hugo making a beeline in their direction.

"What have you two adorable creatures been up to?" his bright eyes enquiring. Without waiting for a reply, his face changed, now a picture of sour scorn. "Can I ask you, why are there so many crusty old fossils here? He shrugged his shoulders indignantly and placed a hand on his hip. "I mean, I like a man with a bit on the clock, but darling...." adding curtly, "Speak to Billy, darling, or it is the last time you'll see me, I'll refuse to come." With a roll of his eyes, he was gone.

They laughed.

Sean shook his head, "Bloody hell, consider yourself brushed down."

Veronica laughed and shuffled in closer, they sat in silence until, "What was going on with you at the funeral?"

Sean looked embarrassed and could feel a flush rising up his neck, he squirmed until he found his ammunition. "What do you mean? It was you kissing Billy that caused it all."

"So what?"

"So what, I thought you were with me, you didn't tell me about you and Billy."

Veronica laughed, raising her hand to her mouth. "Billy and me?" Her head shaking in disbelief. "Billy and me?" "Billy's gay!"

The group nearby raised their heads, looking over.

She lowered her voice to a whisper. "He's gay. I thought you knew. Why do you think he invited you?"

Sean jerked his head back, confused, "I don't know,

THE PICTURE GAME

I'm not gay."

Veronica knocked the side of his head with her knuckles, "Cormac!"

The penny had not dropped.

"Cormac," Sean repeated. There was a glass of wine on the floor, he picked it up, holding it as a shield as his mind raced. "No, that's bullshit, Cormac was there in Amsterdam," he thought. He went to say something, but the thought got lost on its way to his tongue.

Veronica went on, "Didn't you know?" her voice was soft and mothering.

She touched the back of his head, he moved it away.

"How'd you know he's gay?" he asked.

She shrugged. "Maybe he ain't. But then me, Billy, Champagne and Francis are all mistaken."

Sean lowered his head, moving it slowly from side to side. He felt betrayed. He took a sip of wine.

"Surely, he must have known," she thought. But seeing him upset, she waited. "He can't change the way he is." Once again, her hand went to his head, this time he left it there.

Sean took a gulp of the wine and a deep breath, "It's not that," he shook his head. "It's not that."

Veronica leant in closer rubbing his back.

He looked into her eyes, paused, "You know when someone has taken the piss, but you don't even know they've taken the piss."

Veronica pulled her head away, her brow furrowed. "What do you mean?"

"When someone takes the piss," he said.

His meanderings meant nothing to Veronica.

Exasperated, he raised his voice. "Why the fuck didn't he tell me?"

Not quite getting his meaning, "Why the fuck didn't he tell you?"

"Yeah," he shouted.

She paused, mulling things over, she did not want to

208

make a mistake in responding. "Maybe he just felt awkward. Like it wasn't the right time."

"And Billy's queer too?" he blurted out, lowering his head when one of the guests looked up.

Veronica shrugged, smiling and nodding confirmation, "It's no big deal."

Sean sat thinking.

Veronica leant forward and kissed him. "It's no big deal," she repeated.

Sean held on to her, his thoughts went to his brother. "Yeah, no big deal, maybe…?"

35
A New Year

Ma checked her watch. It was five to midnight. There was no chance of Paddy turning up now, she thought. She wiped away a tear and looked over at Aggie.

The crowd were gathering in the middle of the dancefloor, ready for the count down.

Mrs McGarry, led the crowd as they called out, ten, nine...."

The Emerald Five had begun the opening notes of Auld Lang Syne.

Ma let out a sigh, a sigh of resignation. Aggie reached under the table and held her sister's hand.

The navvy wandered across, he spoke in a soft Irish brogue, "Come on ladies, we'll see the New Year in."